Table of Contents

Prologue 1
Rumors 6
Ripples 12
Departing Delevan 23
Shifting 29
Precious Things 36
Appellation of Fae and Lady 90
Wolf Moon 104
Bringing Down the Flowers 111
Edge-Walker and the Gypsy 128
Badb Karma 153
Once in a Blue Moon 167
Epilogue 218
Note from the Authors 220
What Did You Think? 223
About the Authors 224

DELEVAN HOUSE

Ruthann Jagge
&
Natasha Sinclair

DELEVAN HOUSE

JAGGE & SINCLAIR

© 2023 Ruthann Jagge & Natasha Sinclair
All rights reserved. This book or any portion thereof including all images, may not be reproduced or used in any manner whatsoever without the express written permission of the author and publisher, except for the use of brief quotations in a book review. Any unauthorised use will constitute as an infringement of copyright.
https://brazenfolkhorror.com
Contents are works of fiction. Names, characters, and events are the products of the authors' imagination. Any resemblance to actual persons, living or dead, or actual events is purely coincidental.
Original Cover Art by Don Noble, Rooster Republic Press.
Published by Brazen Folk Horror
First published 2023.
Other formats available.
ISBN: 9798215774250
ISBN: 9798360421207
ISBN: 9798360422136

Content Note

Delevan House includes mature themes that are integral to this complex work of genre-bending, dark speculative fiction.

Please be advised that some of the words, events, and acts depicted in this story may be unsettling to some readers.

Dedication

We dedicate Delevan House to all those who believe in and keep the old stories alive. Around the hearth, with sleepy heads on fluffy pillows, with friends, family and strangers who may be oceans or worlds apart. Passing old tales through generations, ever-changing.

Our fables desire to be shared and evolve to reach through the hourglass of time. We hold on to true immortality in the sharing of stories.

Names get lost, language evolves, and landscapes change; stories are the magick that binds us all through history, culture, love, hate and everything in between. Our tales live on long after we are gone—if we are brazen enough to share them.

Tell your stories. Believe in magick. Reimagine, and keep the fire burning! Once that flame is snuffed, there's no going back. There's only the dark.

No one wants to be truly alone in the dark.

Acknowledgments

Neither of us would be able to spread our creative wings so freely without the support and encouragement of our families. And neither of us takes that for granted. Ever.

Especially with a craft as solitary as creating stories can be. Outside literature, we both know what it's like to have our voices oppressed and stifled in an ever-increasingly critical and controlling world.

Where folks feel (un)progressively entitled to be judge, jury and executioner; we've each been the witch or the devil on the other side of pitchforks. To have people in our lives who accept us to the core without questions, without judgement, and with love; there are few things as important in relationships and authentic connections as those elements.

We're two women who have life-long danced to the beat of our own drum(s)—high creatives who choose to live extraordinary lives full of beauty, humor and a touch of mischief.

Ever patient and often, ever amused, Paul and Mike, our ever-suffering partners, are given our deep gratitude in this debut publication from Brazen Folk Horror. When we've not been able to talk things out directly with each other in the design of this book and those to follow, Paul and Mike were at the other end of a bombardment of ideas. And, we are sorry, your earaches aren't over—for this is only the beginning.

"Nicnevin with her nymphes, in number anew
With charms from Caitness and Chanrie of Ross
Whose cunning consists in casting a clew"
—Alexander Mongomerie, 1585

Prologue

Delevan House is the image seared into every mind. The captivating nightmare from which one is too afraid to run. The name on every pair of quivering lips. *Delevan House*.

The grandeur of the building was as exciting as terrorizing and altogether unsettling. The only structure nestled between the serpent and the crow—lochs that (almost) cut her off from the village in which she is so central.

Her construction was more than mere bricks and mortar. She pulsed with darkness from those interred within her. Soaring in the skies above were the Delevan flock, her eyes beyond the iron—a devilry that could barely be contained.

Fear rattles one's heart when one feels the mossy, wild ground that should be still, beating. Standing on the Delevan land, one could feel the pulse of trapped souls. A deep, low—lub-dub... lub-dub... lub-dub. No matter how thick the sole of your boots, stand there, and you'll feel it penetrate your toes, soles and soul—lub-dub... lub-dub... lub-dub.

Regardless of the panic galloping within the living, her beat remains calm.

The appearance of Delevan House was akin to a place of worship, a goddess in stone and glass and all that was a part of the astounding building. She's an exquisite cathedral in miniature.

NATASHA SINCLAIR AND RUTHANN JAGGE

Sharp angled arches tower behind the manor's external walls, its cloak of secrecy. Spires are not unlike those that could be ascribed to gothic architecture. However, that description was newer than Delevan House, which may have been born when the style was more known as Opus Francigenum.

She was spectacular.

Even from distant external glimpses, with her ogival arches, exquisite stained-glass windows, and elaborate tracery, she was unlike anything else standing. The building was graced with ornately decorated flying buttresses that crawled with intensely aromatic night-blooming flowers, some known for their ability to affect living creatures, perhaps even raise the dead, arching over the magnificent internal gardens.

Images were carved into the ancient stone, overseeing all—eyes perpetually watching. Perhaps the most distinctive was the menacing solitary gargoyle perched high above the arched entrance of Delevan House. His face snarls in an aggressive permanence—distinctly unwelcoming.

The gargoyle is the most frightening figure to many of the villagers. Some say it appeared following the disappearance of the Laird in 1667 during the final Great Scottish Witch Hunt. Look closely at images of the Laird, and there is a rugged resemblance to the long-gone landowner of Badb.

The gargoyle crouches on strong muscular legs, with his arms reaching down and hands just ahead of his flat, steady feet, gripping the platform he was perched upon with talon-like claws. Definition ripples, life-like in slate-gray stone, ropey veins pop. Strength exudes from the magnificent carved beast. His face gazes down upon his surroundings—with his strong, sharp jaw, a furrowed brow, and mouth partially open. From his head, ram-like horns rose and curved back, drawing the eye towards his wings, which held the same tension as the rest of his crouching-ready-to-pounce body—a demon hunting his prey. Delevan's great, winged stone beast evoked stalking nightmares of terror in some of the people of Badb and a shameful intense lust in others. He penetrated dreams and nightmares alike, inspiring intense desire and terror in equal measure.

Thirteen monoliths surround the building. Standing stones etched in a language long lost. Many theorized Pictish, though close analysis was impossible unless you were inside. With technological advances, the curious had tried long lenses and drones to capture a closer look. But images always came out blurred, over-pixelated, obscured by some inexplicable cloak over the manor, no matter the weather or tools used to capture the shot.

Old folktales told of a great circle, with a stone altar in the center, where ancient people of the local land gathered to celebrate harvests and lay animal blood sacrifice for the next season's fruits, grains, and meat.

The monoliths pre-dated the house. This was known from the old stories. Back when folks rooted their beliefs in those tales shared by mouth, the land, and her wisdom before the tyranny of the church and other politics stripped nature from them.

Now, the great stone circle enveloped the grounds of the gothic manor house. These 10-foot-high gray, thick-set menhirs were eerie guardians. Few dared go near, only curiously looking from the duckboards that connected the land where Delevan House lay separate from the village. The duckboards were placed between the narrowest point of two Lochs—Delevan Loch on the south-east of the house and Loch Badb on the north-west, known locally as the 'serpent' and the 'crow' due to their distinct and unusual formations. Yes, few dared go beyond the duckboards, though some more ignorant and curious tried.

Encircling the stones, among the overgrowth, was an 8-foot-tall iron fence. An unusual sight in a heavily agricultural territory that was divided using various types of hedging, and this carried through the residential areas. At Delevan House, though, it was said that the iron bound evil there. There was a historic agreement with the village blacksmiths, the Sutherlands, to maintain the fencing. The Sutherland family never failed to tend to their agreements, and such contracts were passed vigilantly from one clan blacksmith to the next in a binding generational commitment.

The rhythms and customs of the surrounding inhabitants were because of this opposing structure dominating their lives. Delevan House was central to their continued existence and had been since the last Laird of the house let the land out to the villagers in the mid-1600s.

Everything in the universe is a slave to biological, chemical, and social rhythms. In truth, there is no such thing as freedom. The idea is a delusion, perhaps the most ridiculous one of all. We're all trapped. We build our own prisons, stone by stone — unknowingly. Born into them and taking up the reigns of those who came before us. The Badb villagers know that better than anyone.

Delevan House was no slave.

She was, however, to be feared.

DELEVAN HOUSE

Delevan House was bound and tended to by an eternal promise made by long-dead ancestors. Rumors of witchery, demons, fae folk, forbidden sorcery, and rituals that must be kept firmly within the walls inspired tension. One that never ceased tightening around the throat of the villagers who lived alongside her, dominating their superstitions and traditions.

The house commanded and oversaw the doings and undoing of every soul of the village, even the unborn—those were a favored delicacy. With her immense, domineering presence, little was truly known. Only words and sigils of protection etched in those menhirs knew the truth, and perhaps the beady mirrored black eyes of the birds that roosted around her.

Although the exterior was astounding for this quaint village of Badb and was a symbol that instilled much fear in the locals, it was those who resided inside that were truly terrifying.

Your journey into the deep-rooted Delevan House and those that forged her heart into the land begins here, in the village of Badb.

Rumors

There are reasons folks avoid the village of Badb. It's not easy to locate. You won't find its name on any maps of the U.K., only stumbling upon it if you're traveling on one of the two rough-paved roads crossing in the center of daily life.

Badb nestles between unnatural bens, formed of eons of mining, and stretches out onto flat planes that reach out to the peat lands overlooking the ragged coastline of steep craggy rock faces that drop mercilessly into the freezing North Sea.

The flat planes of the village lack distinction except for the near-constant clouds of smoke belching foul air into the sky from the raging furnaces on the entrance to the village if traveling north. It's a wonder the land sustains farming as it does. Most would take another road than travel through Badb.

For pilgrims who had experienced the blissful landscape, clear air, and scenic romance of the glorious Cairngorm mountain range, also known as Am Monadh Ruadh, to then be faced with the stench and decrepit nature entering this village, it was akin to crossing over into another world entirely. In otherwise picturesque highlands, one had to wonder how this little slice of stinking hell could exist.

The acrid smell of molten iron combines with the distinctive stench of dust and sulfur, attacking the lungs like a relentless plague. One could feel their building damnation with every breath. Some claim the village is damned, and others believe that Satan himself inhabits one of the old stone cottages, daring the curious or foolhardy closer for a better look. Even the Highland Clearances managed to avoid Badb village, preferring to stay clear of the inbred residents; only the occasional gypsy may take the risk. But those making that choice to lay hearth in there were extremely rare. As rare as a Blue Moon on Samhain.

Badb's past binds those born there; no one would choose Badb; it, however, may choose you. So, those born there remain. Generation after generation. The seams and pockets of the rich black ore run under and around Badb, providing a support structure to the earth, not unlike that of human veins. You can almost feel them when on Badb lands; whispers call to the bones, racing through the fresh blood. For some, it's run. For others, there's a compulsion, a burning poker-hot need, that demands, stay... forever.

Its inhabitants define the word clannish. Small and of a similar mind, they prefer, for the most part, to be closed off to outside influences and opinions, and for generations, leaving or marrying outside of the village has been heartily discouraged. They have their reasons. And Badb bloodlines are thick and deep-rooted, like the industry providing the primary source of employment and income—the mining, processing, and export of their iron.

Badb blacksmiths are renowned for their skill in the forge. The demanding trade is a source of pride for those who learn it, usually at the knee of an experienced family member. The Sutherlands were the village smithies for as far back as records existed. The Sutherland men are stoic, hardworking and burley.

NATASHA SINCLAIR AND RUTHANN JAGGE

The women of the family often shared the same stoicism. Much was kept within the family. And although there were always those astute in business throughout each generation, the Sutherlands did little to blend with those 'outside' their name. Yes, even marriages were kept within. The courting of cousins encouraged them to maintain their elite pool of purity.

The secluded village is the subject of many superstitions, and the locals do little to discourage gossip and whispers that keep away unwanted intrusions most of the time. They had a history of partaking in it, which added to a particularly grisly past.

Pivona McQueeney's pronounced widow's peak accents huge gray eyes blinking with anticipation as she listens with her ear close to the door of a neighbor's shabby cottage. Willowy to the point of frail, the teen has been a familiar fixture on the streets of Badb, an outsider who has made her way in. She prefers absorbing the business of others, lurking in shadowy corners and behind thick hedges, to an acceptable conversation. Her unruly braids are decorated with bits of colored thread and hang beneath a plaid wrap, and the threadbare edges of the wool flutter in the chilly air like tattered brown feathers against her hollow cheeks.

She waves away three audacious black birds circling nearby, fearing their chatter will expose her presence. The creatures are a fixture in the village, sometimes blackening the sky in clusters

DELEVAN HOUSE

of shiny wings and plump bodies, eager to swoop down for a listen or a nibble.

Voni doesn't communicate well with people. Her dialect is a mixture of parts that don't always fit together coherently. Her voice is undeveloped and lacks confidence. She knows that she's different except within the minority in which she was born. Here in the village, Voni connects emotionally to the birds as if she's a member of the flock. They accept her flighty nature, at least, she likes to think so anyway.

Hearsay is Pivona's stock and trade. The offspring of tinkers, who happened upon Badb on their travels, the girl learned how to repeat information with a conviction for profit at a young age. Voni wasn't missed when the gaudy caravans moved quickly on under cover of darkness. She was one less mouth to feed. By abandoning the girl in the village, it left an opening for returning to collect a bounty or dowry on her, depending on how well she and they fared.

The residents of Badb aren't welcoming to strangers. Those who hear about the exceptional skills of local blacksmiths are willing to try their hand at bartering in exchange for precious ironwork skills and trade secrets. Voni's family were swiftly turned away and not too kindly either.

Everyone and every place have secrets. Voni delights in gathering them like bouquets to be offered in exchange for something more valuable to the abandoned young Traveller. Even the persistent birds drop shiny tokens or stolen trinkets at Voni's feet. They depend on her keen sense of hearing for information as well.

NATASHA SINCLAIR AND RUTHANN JAGGE

Some people living in neighboring towns have strong opinions regarding the clusters of black birds darkening the skies. They have opinions about just about everything.

Silhouetted by fast-moving clouds and the branches of pine trees resting in winter's chill, they roost at sunset. Hordes of the winged-gossips cluster in familial groups, gathering in larger murders when a situation, concern, or activity worthy of excitement, requires further consideration. The corvids are taken seriously by those in the village. Some respect them, but more often, they are feared for what they are capable of in the community. The flock never dwindles; it only grows.

The cunning birds are highly social with each other. During cooler months, the birds are less active, swarming together to roost at dusk, then dispersing during the day in search of exciting situations; they are present at every funeral. Much gossip can be found dripping out into the open on gravesides. The departing of young ones sees the presence of the majority of the great Delevan flock as if such death doesn't create enough unease than being surrounded by a great black mass of beady eyes. The gathering and redistribution of signals and snippets at these turnouts allow the black-winged mourners to respond and adapt to the environment. The crows of Badb and their staging areas are protected by an ancient force.

Voni not only listens to conversations and private discussions, but she regards the crows as her co-conspirators in gossip. When she discovers a detail capturing her interest, the girl scratches hasty notations on nearby rocks, using a lump of coal in a unique hand. The smudgy black lines and symbols form an alphabet of sorts, unknown to most humans but easy for the learned birds to decipher. The girl feels they understand

and trust her, although she's not particularly fond of the mistress they are believed to serve.

They gather and roost at *that* house, the one the villagers avoid so vehemently. It's set apart from the rest of the village—an outsider like its birds that some call the Delevan Eyes. The villagers fear them too. Some believe that their mistress's house sprung from the snarled heather, forming itself around the great monoliths. Dark sentinels standing before and within the irons. Others say it was a gift from the devil to the village's powerful witch, who promised her soul in exchange for the innocence of a child or the love of the Laird. Voni has overheard many of the stories.

But she accepts the birds. Birds are a constant no matter where she finds herself, often with little choice in the perceived freedom of her heritage.

Ripples

Winter enveloped the land with blankets of snow, and a ghostly hush befell the village of Badb. There was a distinct icy chill of abandonment.

If a tourist were to find themselves in the village, they would be torn between staying and exploring this strange little place, seemingly unchartered, or leaving as fast as possible. The energy was eerie and unnerving, like a shadow whose source you can't place when you wake in the middle of the night—with inadequate sight straining to make sense in the dark, wondering if something is watching you.

They were watching. They still are.

In Badb, someone is always watching.

Beira, The Queen of Winter, had breathed her magick across the lochs flanking Delevan House, freezing them instantaneously as they lapped against the banks. Halted in time, they became silenced, glassy, mirrored ripples.

The evergreens of Badb forest, located north of its namesake loch, glittered in a frozen crust of white diamonds perched on needles. The naked trees of the dense woodland stretched like elegant giant dancers on pause, frozen in timeless beauty and sinister shadow.

DELEVAN HOUSE

Caoimhe Delevan's birth was witnessed by crows. Guarded, with eyes like portals, black holes to another plane. Feathered cloaks gathered in silent vigil around the buttresses of the house. On all fours in the garden, her mother was nude, palms pushed deeply into the soil. The iron cuffs around her wrists and forearms burned, and her skin felt as if it were aflame. Her feet arched as birth dominated her body. Mauve, a rare-white crow, perched on her shoulder as if the bird was an extension of her mistress. Fraoch, the great black crow—larger than any raven—guarded his Lady from the front. Taking in every convulsion and cramp, he felt everything as she did. Such adrenaline and pain had a different effect on the great bird—nourishing.

He watched. Soaking in his mistresses divine agony.

Lenore had to feel the earth, be buried in the cool dirt as transition gripped her body and soul. She had lived several lives, and a new course was imminent.

Ghostly clouds eerily floated across a thin crescent moon. Silence, but for the soft moans of a lady becoming a mother, alone. The white crow pressed her pink claws into Lenore's skin. Lenore pressed her crown against the cool earth when the stampede peaked and hovered in her lower pelvis. Her body stretched and bloomed like the previous years' roses that blossomed every summer by the front gates. Instinctively, Lenore's body responded, pushing searing hot new life out into the cool night air.

Her child, a child of Imbolc, was born—Caoimhe Liùsaidh Delevan.

Lenore rocked the newborn, slick with blood and perfection, in her arms. "My impossible daughter," she cooed. She truly was—an impossible girl from an impossible mother.

Above, not only were the hungry and curious crows' eyes on the child of Delevan so too was the gargoyle guard. Away from his deep plinth at the front of the house, his great menacing and muscular form observed from above, wings outstretched in fierce protection. This was the first he had moved from his post. The child had cast a spell over every inhabitant of the house.

This child of Delevan was held in secret for several human lifetimes. One day villagers began noticing the vague silhouette of a child through the near-opaque stained-glass windows of the dreaded house. Lady Delevan was no longer alone in her captivity. *That witch has done something*, they'd profess. Perhaps a deal with the devil before her confinement?

Through the rabble of rumors, the child grew as all girls do inside the great walls behind pillars and iron.

Caoimhe filled her mother's deeply tarnished heart with something new, something close to love and a steadfast and fierce devotion. It filled the obsidian flock, too, that love, that vivacious energy. She had something many of those souls longed for—life and the potential for freedom that their wings could never match. The freedom of birds was an illusion to all the world. Only their mistress knew their enslaved reality; her eyes in the sky. Nonetheless, they loved the gregarious, effervescent child of hers. She was their sister.

DELEVAN HOUSE

Caoimhe Delevan was an integral and magical component of the Delevan dynasty, for better or worse. As one of the few whose heart and soul remained in its original vessel, her perceived purity allured her feathered siblings. Growing up in a house of magicks, a home sacred and sentient. It was not merely a building but a living, breathing entity. Encircled by a lush garden of wild evergreen shrubs and flowers, all blooming and dying through the seasons. Surrounded by wild heathers and the great stones that crawled with climbing plants, moss and ivy, a bustling home for birds in a place otherwise void of dense greenery; life teemed from the gray stone.

The girl of the house challenged her mother. She longed for more, begged for more. She pinned and fluttered from wall to wall like a moth trapped in a jar. And she found her escape, eventually, through the curious attentions of Grant Sutherland. The blacksmith who came to fulfill his duty of tending to the iron fencing—the witch's cage.

Time moved differently for the Delevans than it was perceived by most. While the hourglass grains sped like a freight train for mortal beings. For those lucky enough to discover any true wisdom in their short lives, it was always too late. The youth rarely listened to the ramblings of a fossil, as they often saw their elders. Discarding professed wisdom as a last-ditch attempt to leave a mark and be remembered. Perhaps all mortals craved immortality in that sense.

NATASHA SINCLAIR AND RUTHANN JAGGE

When Caoimhe Delevan came to the attention of (and he to hers) Grant Sutherland in 2012, she could have easily been perceived as a young woman no older than 26-years-old. No one could imagine that she was born in 1670. The Delevans aged slowly compared to purebred humans.

Caoimhe's mother used to say that the freckles dancing across her nose and cheeks were kisses from the faeries. She wasn't a regular girl; perhaps neither were those to be found in the freedom of the village. Her mother wasn't using terms of sweet lies. There was truth in her words, always.

Caoimhe was connected to the fae; ancient bloodlines pumped through her veins. Imbuing the girl with magical gifts. Similar to human girls—who came into themselves through burning conflict fuelling irreversible changes in adolescence. Caoimhe, too struggling with her changes and maintaining control.

It's always in the blood; blood changes everything.

Converting sweet to bitterness, casual interests into obsessions, slight annoyance into burning hate. And the Delevan line was particularly potent. Blood infused by the source of all life and death on earth—the Daughter of Frenzy.

As the only child of the great house, Caoimhe had her mother's full attention, who was an extraordinary woman in every sense. Lenore Delevan was tender and sweet with her daughter, though Caoimhe couldn't be sure if she had ever really felt love from her parent. She knew that she cared for her deeply, but the notion of love seemed too petty for the matriarch. And she was that too—as far as Caoimhe was concerned, her mother was her only family along with the house. And the house had hearts like no other. She could hear them beating within the walls—lub-dub... lub-dub... lub-dub.

Lub-dub... lub-dub... lub-dub... beating a lullaby for a solitary child of the dark.

Snowdrops and daffodils began to push through the last snow covering the land. It was Caoimhe's favorite season—the hardness of winter submitting to spring gave her hope. Observing the strength and determination in something that appeared so delicate always brought a smile to her face, followed by a heavy sadness in her heart. She loved her mother dearly, but she, too, needed to break out. Push through the darkness towards a light of her own.

Caoimhe had long devoured the library's contents. As rich as those volumes were, the world had surely undergone many changes since the words she had last read of it. She craved new stories and thirsted to make her own outside the confines of the house.

The landscape around the grounds of Delevan House was untouched, except for the tracks of birds that skirted across the snow like the prints of tiny skater dancers. Like the birds, she wanted to make her marks. Desiring an existence beyond her mother, the birds, the books and the stones.

Caoimhe had watched this Sutherland man and his ancestors before him tend to the fences for hundreds of years. One would die, and another would take over. A promise—an obligation that was passed seamlessly from father to son. None of them had gotten her attention like the current Sutherland smithy. She had watched him from the house windows since he started going with his father as a young boy, learning their family craft. He was such a mischievous, mucky little lad. He would run, circling the wrought iron fencing that closed in Delevan House. She saw his interest deepen as a teenager and his eyes wandering curiously around the windows. But she never let him see her. Now, as a grown man, she flushed, thinking of what it would be like to touch him. More so, what it would be like for him to touch her.

He had seen her by the window once. That she knew. She also understood that her existence might have been shrugged off as an apparition or imagination. After all, no one had seen her outside the house, only behind the glass. She was simply another rumor, a phantom.

Lenore Delevan had long warned her daughter of the villagers and what they had done to her—them. The scars from which she could not heal due to the iron gauntlets welded on her forearms. Lady Lenore Delevan, a once blinding beauty, was imprisoned in her tortured skin. But Caoimhe, like all young women, was compelled to find the truth for herself. She knew that everything, even truths changed over time, and often there was more than one to a story. The crows' eyes assured her so.

One dusk, the dark murder swooped in a majestic performance as they returned to their roosts upon Delevan House and the lone island on the adjacent Badb Loch. The flock was as much a part of the house as the stones that built it, and they were as much a part of Lady Delevan as her bones. Many of them were as old too. Each soul was encased in jet feathers—all-seeing eyes selected by their mistress; her link to the world beyond the iron fences.

Grant Sutherland was tentatively reinforcing the old irons alone. *He really is not like the others*, she mused, peering from her mother's garden room. Even after all these years, their gardens remained lush. The flock always delivered the necessities for their mistress. Well, at least those necessities their feathered forms could manage—all things of value always begin with a humble seed. Caoimhe had become entirely fixated on the movement and strength of Grant's hands. Imagining her body gripped in his embrace as he was gripping his tools. Shuddering a little at the thought. She watched and moved from window to window, tentatively following him from within her walls. This had become her routine whenever she saw the handsome blacksmith.

On this day, she ventured outside, something she had only done in another form. She held her breath and crept, keeping within the boundaries of the ample gardens. Garnering a better viewpoint while trying to keep hidden behind the shrubs and plants.

She stalked him, breathing in his scent that had mingled with the flora. His scent was earth and fire rolled together with spice overtures. It sped her pulse. She closed her eyes and inhaled deeply, trying to capture the essence of this intriguing mortal. Her eyelids fluttered, and her body moistened in response to his scent. She was aflutter. Caoimhe purred. When she opened her eyes, he was staring at her, gawking.

She had lost herself, and now she had been seen by Grant Sutherland, the man whose name she had heard called countless times by his father. In the open. *Shit!* She stood there looking startled, wide eyes staring back at his—a cat caught in the headlights. He composed himself as soon as her eyes caught his.

Smirking, "I've seen you before," he said.

"I know," replied Caoimhe.

"So, what are you doing in there?"

"How do you mean?" she said.

He stood taller and stretched out his arms from being crouched along the fencing, working, she supposed.

"I live here."

"With..." he trailed off, furrowing his forehead, uncertain how to ask.

"Yes. I live with her. She's my mother."

"Your... mother?" He scoffed, "And here, I thought my family were fucked up." He ran his fingers through his jet, swept-back hair, brushing back unruly loose strands that had fallen by the side of his face.

They both laughed a little, breaking some of the tension.

"So, what do you do in there," he asked.

"Same as everyone else, I expect. I read, draw, the usual stuff."

"Ehm. Yeah. Right, I don't think there's much *usual* about your place, no offense," he sniggered, which somehow accentuated his cheeky charm.

Caoimhe flushed. She wanted him to like her and not think her strange. "Well, what is it that you do then? Apart from the obvious tinkering with metal?"

This is how it started. Over the following weeks, Grant found excuses to work at the Delevan property. Saying that he wanted to be sure of its security. No one at the forge or in his family challenged this since it was unthinkable that anyone would spend time near that place unless they had no choice.

They read together with the iron fence between them, taking turns. He started bringing a novel each week—she had read everything in the house and spoke of her boredom. John Irving was among his favorite writers and became one of hers too—big stories about the many small things that make up the color of life, lives outside of a single house, at least. Lives entangling with others in love, misery, lies, and truth. She even envied the misery, though there was some comfort in the loneliness, even if they were fictitious. Her years of angst and frustration of being so stuck and closed off changed with Grant. She was less discontent with her situation because she was filled with a rush of excitement in his presence and anticipating his visits. This wave passed, of course, and she wanted more from him and the world.

"Why don't you come in and stay a while longer?" Her eyes bore through his, deep diving into his blue pools, and he felt her in him.

Wings rustled overhead, black beady eyes watched from the buttresses, tilting their heads in interest. She had never asked that of him before.

"Caoimhe..." he held her cheek in his palm, and she leaned into his heat, "I want to, but you know I can't. I shouldn't."

"But you know things aren't what they say. You know me. They don't even know that I exist." She kept her sparkling marbled jades fixed on his oceanic pools.

"It's not you, Caoimhe. It's—"

"Her." She finished for him, "Grant, she won't."

He cut her off, "You don't know that. She might. It's not long until the ritual. I've seen—"

"Oh, no, you haven't. I don't think any of us really have seen what she can do. That so-called man of God, that goddamn woman-hating sadist, Lawrence Gordon and the rest of the village saw to that. Even your family, Grant. I hate them."

He sighed, exasperated.

"I mean, do you even know what he did to my mother. Do you? Do any of you really know? I'll answer. No. No, you don't."

"You say it like you do. You speak of it like you were there."

"I may not have been there, but I live with her. I know her and her story straight from her lips. Unlike you and the rest of them." Her eyes shone with anger and those jades clouded with storm.

"I don't want to fight. Fuck! I love you! I've never said that to anyone before. I fucking love you, Caoimhe."

"You're just a coward..." disappointment filled her eyes. He felt sick to his stomach to see it.

Grant didn't know then that Caoimhe could leave the confines of the Delevan grounds. However, her appearance was not as he would have expected when she did. One not yet able to be shared with her love. She wasn't ready and couldn't be sure that he was either.

Caoimhe wasn't bound by the same chains as her mother. She was an entirely different animal; her stock was even farther from human than Lady Delevan's. She craved to have him in her territory, even if it was shared with her mother's thirst. She wanted to test his feelings for her. She wanted, no needed, to be the one he would do anything for. In truth, she was the only one in the eyes of the equally infatuated Sutherland boy. A trait she shared with her matriarch was that men and women could not truly refuse a Delevan. Their unique charm also omitted pheromones unmatched by any living thing, making them entirely and maddeningly irresistible.

Departing Delevan
Winter 2013

The stained-glass windows of the sitting room were fogged white in the gloomy morning. The air felt thinner than usual. Caoimhe was picking at her fingernails, a habit from when she was a child, that she did when she had something to ask that she was afraid may upset her mother. Tiny crimson beads rose from where she peeled the skin back too deep. She put her finger to her mouth and sucked, squeezing the oozing wound. She chewed and swallowed the loose skin.

Lenore regarded her daughter from her high-backed, moonstone upholstered chair—as pristine as it was the day it was made hundreds of years earlier. Her handsome Laird was skilled with his hands, and much of the carpentry in the house was his work, with the upholstery commissioned from the Morvens.

Caoimhe didn't know it, but her binds to the house were from the incantations of her mother. Her mother was trapped but still held a force over those that came from her. Her way of shielding her daughter from the trials of the outside world was to bind her. But the time for change had come, and she knew she must let her child go.

"It pains you, my Caoimhe. Your heart is warm for that boy, and it's not only your heart. Your loins burn too. But you crave more than those things."

Caoimhe sighed heavily. Letting out the air she had trapped inside.

"You can leave, sweet daughter, but, for now, I am bound to remain." Lenore lifted a heavy dark-wood box from the table. It was carved in etchings of fae tongue; secrets guarding secrets. It was weighty, but her mother showed no glimmer of strain. She placed the box before her daughter's feet.

"My gift to you, sweet child of mine." Caoimhe regarded the box with intrigue. She unclipped its smooth, oxidized silver fastenings and lifted the lid. Inside, nestled in a swath of emerald velvet, was a large stone block—a stone from the walls of her mother's most sacred space of Delevan House.

"Mother?"

"It's precisely what you need, my special girl, to make a home of your own. Lay it wherever your heart chooses, and it shall become exactly what you need. No tricks. It'll respond to your heart, my daughter, and spread roots for you."

Caoimhe ran her hands around the rough block, her fingers feeling the bumps and cracks of history from her Mother House. The heavy ancient piece was imbued with the essence of Delevan. That piece was a seed that would become a home where she chose to lay it. "Once you've lain your claim to land with this, your familiar from the Mother House flock will journey to you. One of our great obsidian murder."

Silence thickened the air. Even the birds outside were still. Mauve broke the silence, swooping from her high perch, and landed on Caoimhe's shoulder. Mauve's plumage was the purest

DELEVAN HOUSE

white, her beak pale pink and eyes the turquoise blue of exotic waters sparkling in the sunlight. She was part of the Delevan flock but didn't look like her kin.

"It's no surprise Mauve has chosen you, my daughter. She perched on my shoulder for the labor of you. You are doves among the crows." She pursed her lips. She was weak—ailing before a ritual. Even with the strength she gained from a feed, it was never enough to bring her to full power. The years had become harder on Lenore. She was a wraith, her fierceness muted. Her ethereal beauty was concealed beneath the thick scarring of the trials forced on her body by the long-dead villagers of Badb. But something of that still emanated from her presence, a low hum that just needed *something* to blossom again. And Caoimhe wished more than anything, not only for her freedom but her mother's too.

The next morning, from her bedroom window seat, Caoimhe took in the horizon of the trees of Badb Wood, observing the flutters of leaves and wings within the firs as gold light squeezed between the gaps of the thicket. A view so deeply intimate as observed from this very spot in solitude for hundreds of years. Her eye glided over the loch and the small island that was roost to some of the Delevan flock. As her eyes fell upon the trees, the birds lifted into the air in a magical flurry of wings. The birds dispersed, leaving the trees there bare. They looked lonely, those static, rooted dancers of wood. Cold and exposed to unpredictable elements.

NATASHA SINCLAIR AND RUTHANN JAGGE

She was outside the gates when Grant arrived to take her away from Delevan House and Badb village. She wore a charcoal-gray cowl neck jumper, a simple, sleek black pencil skirt that came to her mid-calf, contrasting with her milky pale legs and ankle boots embroidered with flocked feathers and autumn leaves. She had a small tanned-brown case. It looked antiqued, though sturdy. On top of the case, a rectangular box, swathed in thick green wool, was strapped tightly to it. She stood by her luggage like a statue, with her fingers resting on the box. Her eyes sparkled like the sun hitting ripples of exotic warm waters as Grant came into her view.

Grant threw his arms around her in a firm embrace, wrapping her body in his, she returned his embrace, and they kissed deeply.

Overhead eyes watched.

Grant's feet tingled with paraesthesia. He curled his tingling toes inward against the prickling, and his nerves burned as he inwardly pushed through the discomfort rising from the ground through his body; the beating penetrating him, lub-dub... lub-dub... lub-dub. His heart swelled in his throat. He swallowed the dread back hard—the eerie music of Delevan.

"How did you manage it?" he asked, studying her. She looked different somehow. Less fragile than he held her in his sensitive heart. Part of him had locked her inside as this trapped bird. Now, as she stood before him outside the iron he and his family had so tentatively attended for hundreds of years, her cage, his love looked more predatory than he'd seen.

"She set me free," was all she said. Her voice was stern, and it was clear that she did not want to say any more on the matter.

DELEVAN HOUSE

Caoimhe knew the truth could only add complications. She just wanted out of Badb, and he could take her far enough away for her to start writing her own story, not a fable entwined with the house.

Grant didn't ask any more. The subject of Lady Delevan only caused friction between the two young lovers. All he could think about was having her in his arms, in bed, far from here.

"Here." He shuffled a brown battered-looking knapsack from his shoulders. Opening it, he pulled out something folded in fabric and handed it to Caoimhe. "I swear I haven't said anything to anyone. Before you get upset with me."

"Why would I be upset? What is it?" If her skin weren't so inhumanely perfect, her forehead would be wrinkled.

"She just knew. I don't know how." She understood he was just as perplexed as he was anticipating her to be. "Minerva Morven. She lives in the village. She runs the pub—" he paused.

"Go on," she urged.

"She came to me last night when I was leaving the forge. She gave me this and said, 'it's for the Delevan girl. It'll keep her safe. She's not alone. Make sure she knows that no matter what.' It was weird, Caoimhe. I just stood there, gobsmacked. I've no idea how she knew about you or us. I didn't know what to say. Before I could, she rushed off."

He gripped his hands tight in his thick mane of hair, afraid he would upset her. He was in a fret. His knuckles protruding from his fingerless gloves were whitening from his grip.

Caoimhe regarded him for a moment. *He's telling the truth. He can't lie to me.* She unwrapped the parcel, wrapped neatly in fawn linen and tied with red ribbon. She unfolded an exquisitely designed wrap—jade with swirls of sea-blue. It was heavy and warm, hand-embroidered with white birds. Caoimhe wrapped it around her shoulders. She felt safe, poised, ready to take on the whole damn world. And perhaps, she thought, *maybe I'll find my mother's key. Somewhere, somehow.*

Grant picked up her case, and the young lovers walked together hand-in-hand away from the house, over the muddy duckboards towards the road where Grant's car was parked.

From the highest window, with the gargoyle perched above, she watched her daughter walk away. Mauve swooped low, following at the girl's back.

Shifting
Spring 2014

For three glorious months, the two lovers explored every inch of each other. They shared stories and pieces of themselves that neither imagined sharing with another. Neither could get enough of the other's touch—mutually enthralled by their desire and love. Until this Delevan girl, Grant Sutherland was casually detached from women and always honest about his intentions. He had a particular effect that tickled more than mere lust, especially after sharing a bed with the renowned smithy. Of course, women would still fall in love with him. But it was never returned by him. Grant's heart was in his work, working the elements with his hands. His fundamental passion was in metal and fire. Then there came this woman.

This woman should be impossible. He never knew how small his world was until her.

Grant's heart beat as music against her ear. The rise and fall of his broad chest as her head lay on him was heavenly. Desire prickled her skin. Caoimhe moved her leg over his body a little further; the skin of her thigh brushed his cock. The slightest touch and he hardened. She moved her arm around his broad chest, then down his abdomen, towards the jutting of his hips. His skin was cool to the touch, polar to her heat.

I must have him. All of him.

A deep rumble emanated from her. She pulled her body around and straddled his hips. His shaft thickened against her lips, lightly moist in moon blood. Caoimhe's murmurations of desire rumbled deeper. His eyes remained closed, but he groaned and brought his hands to her hips, feeling her move against him. She teased the length of him and her cleft. Her body was clammy.

She felt out of sorts.

Her nerves electrified with an intensity that overrode any thought; her mind clouded in a thick whirlpool of foggy sparks. Her body took control.

Caoimhe's heart raced, and her blood ran hot, pumping to the surface of every capillary.

She pulled her body up, and with it his head, she angled it against her opening and moved against the tip, slowly—coating him in her blood. She moved her body slightly up and down, rolling her hips above him, and grew wetter, working only his head against her lips. His fingers dug into her hips. Grant moaned his desire—low, deep and guttural. Her body quivered in response, and her muscles strained not to plunge him into her when he growled. Those animalistic desires were for her, testing her restraint.

He was hers.

She teased his cock with the roll of her hips above him. The intoxicating scent of her perfume—notes of deep-heady sandalwood, praline and vanilla mingled with the earlier sex.

DELEVAN HOUSE

The musk of her moon blood made him drunk on her. He wanted to be deep inside her heat and invade this wild woman with his all-consuming love.

She couldn't tease any longer. And Grant could barely refrain from throwing her onto her back and pushing himself inside. He groaned, squeezing his eyes shut, tension hardening every muscle.

Caoimhe came down, slamming her lover's throbbing hard-on into her sex, impaling herself on his thick shaft.

She rocked, rose and fell, rocked, rose and fell, rocked, rose and fell. Slow and hard, she maintained the rhythm.

She ground against him, and he dug his nails into her skin, leaving crescent bloody moons in her flesh. Marking her; his.

He then moved a hand round further to finger her ass as she rocked. Caoimhe gasped, panting her approval.

Her body felt on fire; she slammed herself up and down, impaling her pussy with his wood. The smell of their fresh sex filled the room and sharpened Caoimhe's need.

The metallic musk of her blood mingling with his ejaculate and their sweat made her ride him faster. Her hands gripped his hips as she drove him balls-deep into her body. His cock hit her cervix with that edge of pain and magnified her building euphoria.

This man was her drug. *He has to be mine, always.*

She groaned and moaned her rapture, and he rolled his hips with hers. He drew his face up and tongued her pink nipples. Grazing them with his teeth, Grant hungrily nibbled and sucked. Her breasts quivered hot against him. She pushed his broad chest back hard and pinned him to the bed, and she continued bucking her hips as her claws pinned him down, letting him know exactly who was in charge on this ride.

"Fuck. Caoimhe. Fuck," he cried. "You're so hot."

She panted heavier.

Her skin burned.

Sweat tumbled down her reddening chest.

"Caoimhe. Are you ok?" he panted, "Oh, fuck," still panting, but his voice was filling with something other than pleasure.

She continued to moan, her body rising and falling onto him. Blood and sweat spattered their thighs, dark pools glistening with the diamonds of sweat-soaked skin in the moonlight.

Her body began to vibrate.

"Caoimhe!" Grant's voice was panicked, "You're burning up. Stop."

He tried to halt her with his hands, but her body fought against his. She reached around her hips, pulled his hand from her, and threw his arms back behind his head. Her nails were claw-like talons, and they caught the side of his eye as his arms hit the bed. Blood welled and blurred his vision.

"Caoimhe! Stop!" he yelled. But she couldn't hear him. Her face was now nose to nose with his. *What the hell is wrong with her eyes?* Fear poured through him. *Is she possessed? What in the hell!* His mind reeled as her body continued fucking him.

The eyes that stared down at him from her ghostly pale face were the most vivid emeralds. Each slashed through with jet elliptical pupils, an otherworldly glow emanated from her irises. Moonlight poured in from the open window behind him, and the silvery shards flooded her terrifying eyes. *She's got bloody cat eyes.* He thought.

"This isn't right, Caoimhe. Something isn't right."

Her skin continued to burn, searing hot against his. The friction and heat were shifting his pleasure into agony. This physical agony danced with the terror pounding in his galloping heart, which felt like it would burst through his ribs.

He screamed, and as he did, she cried out. Though hers was not of pure agony, nor did it sound like *his* Caoimhe. Her rhythmic, aggressive panting and moaning had turned into a bloodcurdling wail.

The light shifted in the room. More moonlight streamed in as if an overhead lamp had been turned on high. The stark white light bathed her face, and those queer elliptical pupils vanished into emeralds, black consumed by green.

Her quivering breasts stretched to either side of her body as a wound tore down the center of her breastbone like a post-mortem incision was being cut through from the inside out. Blood gushed from the wound. Her wailing intensified. Grant screamed as blood poured from his girlfriend's chest cavity, still tearing open towards her navel while her body was still locked onto his.

This has to be a nightmare. This has to be a nightmare. It's not real. It can't be real. Wake the fuck up! But I can feel everything!

Grant felt as if the air had been sucked from the room. He was in a vacuum of blood and his screams. He was trapped beneath this demon that had been his love while it ripped his love apart from the inside; being showered in her hot blood, steam rose in the chilly spring night air. He lost consciousness.

Grant awoke late into the afternoon. His head was pounding. His eyes were crusted and stung. One side of his face felt swollen and tight. He pulled his hand to his face and winced, hissing. His left eye and cheek throbbed. *Stitches?* He blinked to clear his vision, and he peered down. A light cotton blanket covered him. The rest of the bed had been stripped. He lay on a bare mattress.

Caoimhe was gone.

All evidence of her was gone.

He was alone.

Grant spent weeks searching for her. Retracing their steps back to all the places they had been since leaving Badb. Spending desperate nights alone with memories of being entangled in Caoimhe's body. He came up empty. No one had seen this exotic-looking girl that he described. Not a whisper of her was to be found.

As mysteriously as she had entered his life, she had vanished.

Grant didn't even have a photograph. She never let him take one; she was 'camera shy.' she'd say. 'You don't need a picture when you have me,' she'd add. But he didn't have her.

Alone, with a gash on his face and a crater in his heart. He could not understand what had happened that final night before her disappearance. A nightmare that couldn't have been real. After all, there was no body, blood, or trace of her—dead or alive.

DELEVAN HOUSE

Though, she was from *that* house. She was a Delevan. In that, he found a peculiar sense of hope.

Grant Sutherland did the only thing he could do and returned home.

He didn't know what to tell folks when he returned. He kept things vague when he said anything at all. He was heartbroken, and the villagers knew his disappearance was to do with a girl—wasn't that always man's downfall. Poor Grant had been led astray by his Eve—a test, some would surmise. He tried to speak to Minerva, who comforted him like a mother but offered no answers. She knew more than she would ever say—that he understood.

His best friend, Robert Gordon, didn't understand the notion of love, as much as part of Grant wanted to confide in him. His lack of empathy and deep familial ties to the binds of Delevan and Badb traditions created a wedge between them that there was no overcoming.

The wheel turned through the years, and Grant did not *see* Caoimhe.

Though, the same could not be said for her.

He was marked, and her obsidian-slashed emeralds would be lurking, here and there, in the dark.

Precious Things

2020

Jenna McCray is a unique and intelligent beauty. Tall and slender with narrow hips and long legs, her features and physique are delicate. Under a cloud of rich amber hair and dark eyes, a narrow nose, distinctly pointed, adds to her ethereal appeal. As an independent young woman, she carries herself with quiet confidence. She can wear anything as if her cheap threads are the finest couture, and strangers often comment on her model-like presence. In truth, Jenna owns nothing that isn't second-hand or purchased at a discount outlet.

Growing up in a large, broke-as-hell family in a small town in Upstate New York didn't allow for conceits or egos, and in her formative years, she preferred the company of book characters to humans. As a child, Jenna was often unnoticed except as an annoyance or expense. The setting of her hometown and the seasons nourished her, with lakes to enjoy in the summer, glorious autumns of changing colors, and frigid winters giving way to springs bursting with flowers and new life.

She had trundled through the motions of an ordinary life, attending a cookie-cutter public school, trying to fit in (which she never did) while navigating the complicated waters of a home plagued with abuse and neglect. Too many personalities and needs were crammed into a small house where no one thrived.

Jenna could never find her place among others. The girl frequented lonely corners making herself small, with a book in her hand and a stolen apple for dinner. Jenna focused on learning and absorbing unusual details of life that others disregarded.

Awkward and intense, Jenna spent her free time in the dusty library, hidden behind a pile of books, or wandering through a small local cemetery, reading the crumbling tombstones, and concocting stories about those who rested beneath weeping angels and granite lambs. Her senses are unusually keen, and although she is the oddity among her family and peers, her exceptional intelligence and uncommon beauty drew some to her, including the birds who guarded her favorite long-dead friends.

"What would you like me to read today?" She'd say as she plopped down on a soft bed of pine needles near the entrance of an ornate mausoleum. Her favorite spot. Jenna pointed to three books spread on the ground. She leaned back slightly and giggled when a large crow swooped in and landed on her worn copy of 'Little Women'.

"Good choice. There's lots to like in this story." Three of the birds perched on a nearby headstone. Heads tilted to the musical sound of her voice. They were always content to listen as she read. And she was only too happy to indulge them.

Jenna struck out on her own early in life to indulge her love of adventure, acquired from hours of reading—a seasoned and dedicated armchair traveler. There was no time or money to indulge in higher education, so she worked long hours at demanding jobs with low pay to maintain a bare apartment and a rusty old unreliable car.

Relationships came and went. Men were attracted to her looks and found her intriguing but challenging—too challenging. It's hard to connect with someone whose emotional wall is rock-solid, and relationships require more emotional effort than the girl was capable of. Parts of Jenna McCray were buried deep. Survival comes in many forms, and she lived a solitary life until she crossed paths with Layton Walker.

Jenna's uncommon sophistication led her to a coveted position in the design and art world. History in all forms is a passion. Jenna's memory was finely honed, and she could recite obscure details enthusiastically.

This landed her a position in an art gallery. The position satisfied her inner scholar and being able to balance her bank account to the plus side for the month was a welcome relief after so many lower-paid jobs.

One afternoon, while dusting objects in the gallery, the surly dark landlord of the property noticed her.

"Your boss is late with this month's commission payment." Layton Walker is a man of few words.

"She's away on a buying trip, but I will let her know you came by."

"I didn't ask you to leave a message. I want my money." He's wearing a tailored gray overcoat, and his glossy black hair falls precisely over the collar with a flick of his hand. He's annoyed. Layton's hooded blue eyes are unsmiling, and his perfect smile is feral. Jenna is uncomfortable being alone in the room with him. Although it was late October, the air was dense. It was hard to breathe.

"I'm not authorized to write checks. There's some cash in the petty cash drawer for minor expenses. Will it hold you over until she's back in town? I don't know what else to say." Jenna's nerves were on edge, and her skin prickled in goosebumps. *This guy is dangerous.*

"It won't do a damn thing or make a dent in what she owes me." Layton moved closer to the willowy young woman. Although attractive, she was not his type. However, her stare was unflinching and brazen, which intrigued him.

"Here's the thing. We will have dinner together and discuss what I expect from this gallery arrangement. I could rent out the space for three times as much and don't need some flighty female thinking I am easy to deal with. I'm not." Jenna chewed the inside of her cheek, trying not to panic or tear up. "Be at this address at seven-thirty, or I'll be back tomorrow with a locksmith." She nodded, shuffling in place as he walked out the door. Although intimidated, she didn't want him to leave. *This isn't me. Who is this guy?*

Layton Walker was a thug in gentleman's clothing who grew up hard on city streets. The product of God-fearing parents who stayed together for the sake of their children while almost killing each other in drunken rages. He learned how to negotiate for what he needed and took what he wanted before dropping out of school as a teen. A ruthless and unforgiving natural predator, he built a reputation on a thick foundation of fear and respect in his home neighborhood and beyond.

A mandatory stint in the military provided access to people and illegal and profitable opportunities involving minor risks. By the time he served his contract, Layton had access to an international network of drug distributors, weapon exchanges, and personal contacts of criminals at the top of the bold enterprises in his pocket. Unscrupulous and fearless, he had built an impressive portfolio of investments that included prime commercial real estate. The helipad built on the roof of the building he discreetly occupied was frequently used to his advantage. Layton seldom stayed in one place or with anyone for long.

In Layton's world, money buys everything, keeps secrets, and guarantees privacy. He employed old friends from his former neighborhood—his way of giving back to the community in opportunity and employment. Even if it wasn't on the up and up. They kept him updated on local activity, enforcing where necessary and were loyal to a fault. Several dealt in stolen goods, and they paid law enforcement to ignore trucks moving under cover of darkness. Their close connections with reputable jewelers and purveyors kept the business ticking over without trouble. Layton was a respectable presence. He donated generously to his mother's church, the less fortunate, and scholarship funds, but still, he was a hardened criminal, nonetheless.

DELEVAN HOUSE

Dinner with the uncompromising man uncovered new feelings in Jenna. The cozy Italian restaurant owner was attentive and gracious, escorting the couple to the best table in the crowded dining room. Layton expertly ordered expensive wine and their meals. He was brilliant with a sarcastic wit and steadfast interest in her naïve exposure to the world. They discussed books while they ate. Layton was impressed with Jenna's conversation skills. Her eyes lit up, and her hands fluttered when she spoke. She was different from his usual companions.

"I need to be in Miami next week, pack a small bag, and be ready to leave early." His fork slid through the air as Layton finished his rare steak. "If you need something, we'll get it there." Jenna's mouth dropped open. Her Crème Brule dribbled onto her chin.

"Miami?!" Layton was amused by the shock in her voice, although he didn't smile. "I don't have a bathing suit." Realizing how ridiculous she sounded, Jenna flushed red and dropped her filigree dessert spoon.

"It will be fun, and I think you'll enjoy the trip." Layton sized up the girl. *She's precisely what I need.* She would add to his appearance of credibility and class. "I'm not married. You're young, free, and single. Is there a reason to say no?" Feeling overwhelmed, Jenna nods in agreement.

Miami is a whirlwind of sand and salt, long walks on a secluded beach, rare wines, and decadent food. He was everything Jenna had dreamt of when it came to a partner and sex. She had been with a few men, but there was nothing fumbling about this one's skills. Layton was calm and present with the charming young woman. For the first time he could remember in years, he enjoyed her company and her ripe body, which was always so ready and responsive to his.

When the small plane landed back in New York, Layton's shoulders stiffened. He dropped her hand and folded his casually in his lap. Jenna gulped back tears. *Why did I think this would be anything else?*

"Thanks for the company." Layton's eyes were empty as he helped her to the door with her bag. The entrance to her apartment complex is plain compared to the luxury hotel they had left. The air was chilly, and Jenna felt the cold in her bones.

"It was great. Thanks for inviting me." Layton brushed her cheek with his lips, flipped the collar of his leather jacket then walked briskly back to the waiting car. Without another glance in her direction, he was gone.

Jenna struggled into her lonely apartment with her bag. The harsh light illuminates her shabby home, "Home sweet home," she sighed, her voice echoing around the bare walls. Her voicemail was full of admonishing messages from her family and an angry tirade from the gallery owner, who was back in town, informing her she was no longer needed. Jenna laughed.

DELEVAN HOUSE

She'd tasted what it meant to live well and wanted more. *Needed more.*

Jobs were scarce at the end of the year. Jenna resorted to sampling perfume at a department store and carrying drinks at a neighborhood bar on the weekend to make ends meet. It wasn't enough. In her limited spare time, Jenna packed her belongings. She had to find a less expensive place to live, and the thought overwhelmed her to tears. She was wiping away weeks of self-pity when there was a knock on the door.

Pushing back the heavy brass deadbolt, Jenna opened the door an inch and peeked cautiously through wet eyelashes into the hallway. Living alone was challenging, and she seldom shared her address.

Layton Walker's cheeks flushed, and his eyes narrowed as Jenna slid the door open wider.

"Are those tears of joy? You're happy to see me?" His hand wedges between the door and her body. "At least you didn't slam it shut. Can I come in?" Jenna nods, glancing frantically around the half-furnished room.

"Going somewhere? I wasn't aware you lost your cushy job until today. I've been busy. I gave the bitch who owns the gallery thirty days to vacate. It was a shit move to fire you. I'd say it was my fault, but maybe not." Layton's icy eyes glitter. "I see you aren't partial to the finer things." He scanned the room. Jenna picked at her chipped nail polish.

"I have to find another place to live, and money's tight. I don't expect you to understand." She kicked a small pile of neatly folded clothing on the floor. "Why are you here?"

"I wanted to see you. Now I'm offering you a job. It includes a place to live, and you'll have me for a boss." His hand on her arm was cool and dry. Jenna shivered under her thin shirt. "Finish packing up what matters, and I'll send someone to help in the morning."

"What will I be doing?" Jenna's eyes are wide. She won't turn him down.

"This and that. Phone calls and paperwork. Meetings and appointments. Travel with me from time to time. As long as you follow directions and don't ask questions, it will be easy." Jenna nodded her agreement and excitement. Anything was better than her current situation.

"I'm serious. No questions, and you'll have a good life. Do as I ask, and keep your mouth shut unless I ask for your opinion or advice."

"Thank you. I'm grateful for the offer. The past few weeks have been hard."

"Why didn't you call me?"

"I don't have your number."

Layton leaned in and pulled the slim woman close. He kissed the top of Jenna's messy ponytail. He lingered for a minute. Jenna wanted to wrap her arms around this stranger for a repeat performance of what they'd shared in Miami. Something about him forbade it, and her wanting arms remained submissive by her side.

"Doesn't matter. You have my attention now. I'll see you soon. Gerry will be by tomorrow to load your things and help you." Once again, the man in the black leather jacket left her alone with questions she was afraid to ask. Jenna spent most of the night sorting and bagging as she scrambled to organize the smallness of her life, which was about to change.

The weeks were a whirlwind of excitement, Layton's invitation brought her into his business world, and for the first time, Jenna was a good fit. His office staff respected her level-headed approach to problems, and she earned their trust. Her salary was more than ample, and she no longer struggled for anything she needed or desired. Her small, well-appointed apartment was dressed in polished antique furniture and decorated with one-of-a-kind colorful art pieces. Her wardrobe was a fashion editor's dream.

"Do you love me?" She dared ask the intense, handsome man who guarded his holdings and heart with ferocity.

"As much as I can. This is the best I have. Take it or leave it." Layton gently pushed her off him one night after wine and a game of backgammon. "Don't expect more. You'll be disappointed." They were often together, and he frequently spent the night, although Jenna wasn't included in the details of his business operations. She knew that not everything he managed was legitimate or legal, but she chose not to give it much thought.

"I am leaving for Europe tomorrow. I expect you will understand."

"Of course. For how long?" Jenna usually accompanied Layton out of the country, although she spent most of her time alone while he conducted business. He liked her to represent at dinner parties—small talk wasn't his best feature.

"Do not ask. You know this. There's a box on the desk in my office. I need you to bring the contents to the guy downtown. You know how to contact him. Do this immediately. It's an unusual transaction, but he'll know how to proceed." Jenna's duties included gathering appraisals and approving sales of valuable items Layton acquired during his many international arrangements. Art, jewelry, and the keys to vehicles and properties were common. His methods of disposal varied, and Jenna handled this efficiently and discreetly. If she went through the proper channels and connected to people he knew and approved, she didn't consider it abnormal or outside the law. Nothing in Layton's world was typical.

"Okay." Jenna bit her lip hard to avoid protesting. "Is there anything else?" She sensed the fragility of their relationship. It was always subject to his needs and moods. Layton poured another glass of wine and drank it quickly. He wasn't himself.

"I'm going to be honest because I value you. I'm meeting someone I used to love while I'm there. I won't promise you there will be times like this when I return." Jenna's hands trembled. Her head sank low as she blinked back tears.

"Stop. I've never said we're exclusive, or for that matter, that you're more than an asset as an employee to me. I'm not your fairy tale ending." Layton's voice was cold. He wasn't her lover—he was her boss. "I have an early flight. There's an envelope with cash in my office, next to the box. Use it to do something for yourself while I'm away." Jenna wanted to cry, she was used to being ignored, but this was another level of disregard. She realized she was disposable. Just as she was with everyone, even her family. Jenna watched Layton dress—it was obvious she was nothing to this man. He was a predator, and she was willing prey.

She turned from his kiss goodbye. He laughed, but his face was as emotionless as the day they met.

"Playing hard to get doesn't work with me, sweetheart. I don't have time for your feelings. Save them for someone who cares." Jenna held back from slamming the door as he left. As she slid the lock into place, she kicked the door, hurting her foot. Limping into a chair, the young woman collapsed in tears. Her future was uncertain once again.

It was still dark when Jenna's unique code slid open the door to Layton's office. She hadn't slept—anxious to discover what he had left for her to contend with. His office was sleek and minimal, with an expensive steel and glass desk in the center of the room—the seat of his power. A carved wooden box rested next to a white envelope containing several thousand dollars in large bills. She gasped and thumbed through the money. Jenna had never held so much in her hands before.

Layton's handwriting on the envelope was a scrawl. Like most things he did—messy: 'For you when you finish the job.'

Jenna gathered the bills into her oversized leather bag.

The carvings on the box were uniform in size and circular in shape—lines and swirls, numbers, and backward letters. Squinting closer, she couldn't make out the language, but the scratches in the dark wood appeared symbolic. Jenna pushed in on the clasp and held her breath.

Nestled within a luxurious bed of deep-green velvet rested an ornate necklace. The pendant was a substantial teardrop wrapped in what looked like an exquisite silver rope design, which also formed the chain. The piece was cool in her hand, and the green stone in the middle gleamed with a rich depth of color. Weighing it in her hand, it was heavy. Jenna had never seen a gem like it—with a marbled appearance at first glance and a polished emerald shine. But gazing a little closer, it was as if she peered into a galaxy of stars trapped within the stone—mesmerizing and bewitching. She shook herself and continued regarding the rest of the piece. The ornate clasp was shaped like a bird. Jenna sniffed, wrinkling her nose. The air in the room was heavy with a metallic scent. *It smells like something died in this damn box.* She replaced the necklace and carefully closed the lid. The obvious value of the item made her nervous.

Another small red leather box lay on the desk. Jenna was surprised at how solid it was when she picked it up. Flipping back the lid, she gasped again at the incredible ring inside. A substantial oval-cut diamond shooting sparks of light, flanked by triangle-shaped glittering black diamonds on either side. Intricate gold work suggested it was an antique, and she couldn't resist sliding it onto her ring finger. It was a much smaller size than she wore and only fit to the first knuckle of her ring finger. Jenna squeezed back tears. One fell on the diamond, reflecting her sadness as she sobbed. It was not intended for her.

Layton's ringtone sounded on her phone, but she didn't answer.

Sliding the incredible ring back to rest in the plush satin, Jenna waited for the tone announcing a message.

"Jenna. I was in a hurry this morning. I left something important behind. Gerry will come by the office to pick it up

DELEVAN HOUSE

and send it to me via courier today. If you're there first, ignore the red box on my desk, it's not your concern. Take the item in the wooden box to the man downtown and deposit the cash he gives you." His tone is aggressive, without so much as a greeting or goodbye. Jenna realized then that for months, she was an expediter for this man, ensuring he wouldn't be caught fencing rare items and antiquities. Signing her good name on documents and taking responsibility for shady business dealings. He didn't care about her position or if she ran into legal issues, as certain accounts were in her name. She had done everything he had asked and gave herself to him as a bonus. *It's my own fault, and I've been a fool.* Layton had used her completely.

Jenna shoved the wooden box into her tote bag. She flinched as the dry wood splintered, and the necklace fell to the floor. *I don't care. Screw you, Layton Walker. I'm not your bitch anymore.* She knew what he was capable of but decided to resign her position, effective immediately, and leave everything he represented and the life he offered behind. Scooping up the ornate ropey silver chain, Jenna fumbled with the delicate bird clasp, then fastened the necklace securely around her neck. It vibrated slightly against her skin before nestling between her breasts. *This thing feels like it has a pulse.* She shook off the notion and focused on her leave. She considered grabbing the red leather box with the expensive ring but doing this would ensure someone followed her. She knew too much. The necklace was warm now, heavy around her neck, and oddly comforting as she eased Layton's office door shut for the last time.

Jenna McCray has a plan.

NATASHA SINCLAIR AND RUTHANN JAGGE

Hurrying down the spiral staircase, Jenna saw Gerry's black sedan through the window as it pulled up to the curb. He was an enforcer. A man devoid of emotion and without morals or scruples. She wasn't having a discussion with him today. She didn't trust him or Layton not to harm her. Frantically tapping the button to the elevator leading to the basement and the way out through the back door of the building, she considered her options. *There's nothing in my apartment I need, and I have enough cash in my bag to start fresh. My passport is in my bag.* Gerry's bulk caused him to move slowly towards the entrance, and she was confident she could make it to the parking lot behind the office.

Knowing she won't be missed, tears welled again, but Jenna bit her lip and shrugged off her emotions as she eased into her white sports car. She'd leave it in long-term parking at the airport; it also belongs to Layton. Once she was several blocks away, Jenna parked at a busy discount store and then pulled out her phone. She would dispose of it at the airport and grab a pre-paid model, ensuring Layton or anyone else was unable to reach her. Clicking through the apps on her phone, Jenna's mind raced with possibilities. *Where can I go to find some peace and give myself time to sort out the rest of my life?* She was not interested in beaches, and the complexity of a large city was overwhelming. *Where then?* The words of a lullaby her grandmother had sung when Jenna was a child ran through her mind, and she stopped clicking.

Scotland. I'll go to Scotland.

She's an expert at booking flights and accommodations and will pay for in cash. Jenna knew from experience that staff can be bought, regardless of the reputation, so she scrolled quickly, scanning Air Rentals by private owners, then selected an address. She booked a month at the location. *It will be enough time to figure out my next move.*

Jenna nervously chewed at her manicure and was anxious to leave. The first flight out departed in three hours. If she was lucky and careful, she would be on that plane.

Jenna hurried into the store, grabbing comfortable leggings and a black hooded top, along with a toothbrush and a few snacks. She slammed through the gears as she made her way to the International Airport a few miles away. Jenna couldn't resist giving the tire a final kick, wishing it was Layton when she scrambled out of the parking garage into the terminal.

The agent at the counter didn't question the cash payment. Jenna convinces her she needs to get to her dying relative overseas as soon as possible and can't find her credit card. She squeezed out a few tears and folded an extra few hundred into the woman's hand. The agent smiled as she discreetly pocketed the bills.

"I travel light." Jenna shook her head and pointed to her designer leather tote bag when asked if she wanted to check in her luggage. The burly handler grinned. Jenna breezed through security with her first-class ticket, bought a pre-loaded phone at a kiosk and a few magazines, and then found a quiet corner of the busy lounge to rest before her flight boards. A quick stop in the ladies' room to crush her old phone under her heel, then discreetly wrapped the remains in toilet tissue. She deposited her past into a tall wire wastebasket on her way out. She was clammy from the light sheen of nervous perspiration under her clingy black clothing but also exhilarated for the adventure ahead. *This is me over you and your bullshit, Layton Walker. Find another dumb bitch to do your dirty work.*

Once on board, Jenna sunk back into the cushy seat and adjusted her dark sunglasses to block out the light and curious eyes. The unusual necklace felt suddenly tight around her neck. The chain could be fibers of rope, strangling her like Layton did. She gave it a gentle tug, adjusting the chain, then pulled her hand back sharply. The medallion felt hot, and it scorched her fingers. Jenna licked them and blew gently to cool the sting. The necklace tightened. Ignoring the strange feeling, *it's just my darn nerves. Just chill,* the young woman eased back into the softness of a complimentary pillow, accepted a glass of red wine, and within minutes, Jenna McCray was asleep, hurtling through the clouds toward her destiny.

The announcement that the plane was preparing to land boomed, waking Jenna with a start from her dead sleep in the sky to a cascade of sideways, pelting rain and thick low-slung blue-gray clouds. Her concept of what time it was shot.

Inverness Airport was a far cry from the life she had lived before. She had never been to an airport so small. It was hard to believe that this little strip was a city airport. She imagined a city of hills and sheep—the opposite of the tightly packed, bustling of New York. Inside the terminal, Jenna perused the various leaflets, boasting the attributes of the gateway to the Highlands—castles, award-winning whisky tours, historical battlefields, museums, The Glenfinnan Viaduct, excursions to

DELEVAN HOUSE

the islands, including the only thing she knew about the city of Inverness—tales of its mythical water beast. Apart from the Loch Ness monster, she knew nothing about this place. When looking at *photographs* of the mythical beast captured on film and the cartoon depictions of the green monster, Jenna was reminded of a story she was told when she was little, one that featured this Nessie. A story that told of treasures buried deep within the vaults of Urquhart Castle, which overlooked Loch Ness, guarded by a terrifying and ancient sea creature, a giant serpent-like monster that patrolled the waters. Her grandmother even told stories of Scotland from as far back as the Painted People—the mysterious great warriors of the highlands—the Picts.

Remembering these tales made her feel a little less out of place here. As though she was with her somehow, singing her lullabies. We're all foreigners, really, even the ancient people of this land now. History becomes foreign even to those whose blood courses with it.

While reading one of the tourist pamphlets, it was stated that Inverness in Gaelic translated to 'mouth of the River Ness.' It struck Jenna that she had run from America, straight for the romanticism of the mouth of another beast. *It couldn't be worse than my fate had I stayed*. Here she could start afresh. She could be anyone.

Jenna finds a seat to retrieve her notebook securely packed in her tote. She needs the address of the bed and breakfast and fumbles for the cash, too, so she can exchange it before leaving the airport. The deal is never as good as with the banks, but there was no time before the flight.

She makes her way through the small terminal, following the signs for the taxi rank. The automatic doors part, welcoming the icy cold to slap Jenna's cheeks. She crosses the road towards the luminous yellow sign marking the rank. A dozen cars are lined up, waiting. Jenna opens the door of the first car, a black Skoda. She's hit by a wall of dry heat as she gets in, shoving her bag on the seat by her side. The overpowering scent of powdery, chemical lemon sherbet air freshener makes her sneeze. "Excuse me," she says, taking a tissue from her pocket and wiping her nose.

The driver clears his throat, "Where can I take you?"

Jenna unfolds the piece of paper and hands it to the driver. "Could you take me here, please?"

He reaches over, taking the address. His fingers are rough when they graze hers. He's not always driven for a living. His hands have known hard labor. The driver screws up his brow, "Lass, yer going tae have tae give me more tae go on. This is no B&B I've heard of, and I know most of them up this way—and there are many. Dae ye have a postcode?" he asks, handing the note back to her.

"Well, no, I don't. That's all I have. It was the address the landlady gave me when I booked it."

He sighed and rubbed his forehead.

"Do ye have a phone number for the place? Maybe that would be worth a wee ring."

"Oh. Yes, let me have a look." Jenna rummages through her bag. Pulling out her notebook, she flips through for the number and then makes the call. The driver watches her in his rear-view, noting her scattered disposition. He wonders what brought her here, alone and seemingly clueless about where she is going. *The young these days—so flighty*. She's scrawling a new note and hangs up.

"Sorry about that. I must have taken it down wrong. Here it is." Jenna smiles awkwardly, handing him the address.

"Right, this postcode can only be one place. Ye sure this is where ye want tae go?"

"This is where the landlady said to go. I've already booked. It seemed nice enough."

"Okay, then, no bother."

She pulled her seatbelt on as the taxi pulled out of the airport.

The ride through a landscape so unfamiliar was both exciting and terrifying. Hills and nothingness loomed in the dark once they had driven through the bright lights of the dull and wet city. She could not shake the paranoia of being followed, glancing out the windows on her left and right. The taxi filled with dry heat, reminding Jenna just how exhausted she was. Although she had slept on the flight, her body felt like it had been awake for days. Her eyes fluttered and closed with her head leaning against the cool of the window.

Jenna woke with a start, her cheek raw from being pressed against the cold glass. The driver eased slowly through the village of Anand.

"Ahhh, there she is," he said jovially, smiling at her from the mirror. "Ye obviously needed that wee nap there."

Jenna yawned, rubbed her cheek, and gave herself a little shake.

"Oh, I'm so sorry. I didn't intend to fall asleep."

"Don't worry about it, pet. It wasn't the most exciting of drives anyway. That's us just came into Anand village now, which is where the postcode you were given takes us."

"It sounds about right. It did look like a small place online." Jenna noticed that a few places appeared to be open. She didn't see anywhere to eat, and now she had slept, her stomach growled.

"The rest of the address has me stumped. And I've been driving these parts for ye on thirty-odd years, pet. Are ye sure this is where ye want dropped off?"

"Yes, if this is the postcode as you say, then I'm sure someone around here can direct me. It doesn't look like a big place?"

"Aye, Anand is a wee place. Someone is bound tae know. Will here do ye?" He pulled up by a row of single-story cottages that led down towards a harbor.

"Sure, this will be fine. Just need to stretch out a bit now." Jenna holds a crumpled wad of bills out to the driver. Frowning, he tries to hand several back, but Jenna holds up her hand. "Take it. I'm grateful for the ride and the help."

"Too much, pet. I can't take that. Are ye sure yer okay being left here? It's not usual tae drop a young lady off in an unfamiliar place where she doesn't know anyone. I wouldn't be happy if you were my daughter."

"I'll be fine once I'm warm and have something decent to eat. I'm a big girl. No need to worry. Thank you." The concern of the stranger was peculiar to her. She's not used to anyone giving her needs or situation much thought. He takes a pencil and pad from his glovebox, scrawls a number, and hands it to her.

DELEVAN HOUSE

"Here, just in case you need picked up, here's my number. It's Harry, by the way." He smiled again, showing his unease at leaving her here.

"Thank you, Harry. I appreciate it. But honestly, I'll be fine."

He nodded, shoving the money into his pocket. Jenna grabbed her bag and exited the taxi. Harry tipped his wool cap, then headed back the way they came.

Jenna suddenly feels very alone. *Maybe I should have gone back to Inverness. Where the hell is this damn B&B!* She wavers for a moment before reminding herself that she would perhaps be more easily found in a city. *Not worth the risk,* she concludes.

Jenna McCray's body feels heavy and sluggish as if all the adrenaline of her escape is catching up with her. She's light-headed too. Squinting at her handwritten note, she tries to memorize the address of the apparently hard-to-find bed and breakfast. She cusses quietly as she looks around at the strange location she has found herself in—a far cry from the hustle, bustle and color of New York City. *Jeez, people actually live in places like this.*

Her shoulders are hunched against the chill. *There's no way he could be on my tail already. Calm down. You're free now*, she tells herself, unconvinced. Jenna blinks, then wipes at her eyes, hoping her surroundings will look more like the dreamy photos in the rental listing. The dense mist coating her eyelashes makes everything appear hazy and mysterious, but the decrepit cottages and cracked pavement are obvious, despite her optimism. The street corner where the cab dropped her off stinks of salty sea air and dead fish, and the narrow street running through the middle of town looks like an abandoned movie set framed with clapboard buildings in need of repair and crumbling fieldstone facades.

A few locals rush to warmer places, huddle under dark hoods and fly-away umbrellas, avoiding eye contact with the attractive young woman, but a man wearing a heavy knit jumper, ragged wax jacket and flat cap shuffles to her side.

His face is weathered. Lines cross his skin like deep rivers, but his blue eyes twinkle. "Are ye lost then, hen?" His voice is gruff gravel, and his accent a thick mumble. He reaches to help Jenna steady her bags, and she notices three fingers are missing from one hand. Jenna tries to control her revulsion at the peculiar stranger, but his rank odor isn't helping. "I can direct ye if yer needin' tae know a place." She clutches her bag tightly. As he moves closer, Jenna repeatedly taps at her phone, trying to bring up the information she needs.

"Piece of shit." She holds her phone up to the gray sky, water dripping down her hands into her sleeve. Nothing. Jenna fumbles inside her jacket and then unfolds a damp scrap of paper. "I'm looking for 726 Orkney Way, the bed and breakfast there. I've been traveling for hours and I'm soaked to the skin." Her hair, an unusual shade of light copper, is plastered to her face and neck, and her hands are wrinkled and wet. There are blue arcs of fatigue under her eyes. She's underdressed for the weather in light leggings and a hoodie, with only a light jacket to keep out the sharp wind.

His teeth chatter then click into a grin, and she catches a whiff of seawater caressing her tongue when he leans in too close for her comfort to look at the piece of paper she's clutching.

DELEVAN HOUSE

"It has four stars and is said to be comfortable, and I need a quiet place for a while." Glancing at the address scrawled on the paper, one of his singed and wiry eyebrows shoots up. He shakes his head.

"Naw, hen. There's nae such place. A'm born n' raised in this toon, and I can say ye won't find it here."

Jenna instinctively reaches for the pendant around her neck and thoughtfully caresses the antique silver, running her thumb around the most unusual green marbleized stone encased within its center. The design has the vague appearance of Celtic knotwork, woven of silver rope. It was an intriguing piece that reeked of history and magick. Fingering the cool surface calmed her; it was almost hypnotizing—enthralling.

She considers her situation through travel-weary confusion in this strange, remote place. *I need to rest and regroup. Anywhere out of the elements will do at this point.*

"Do you know of any place nearby that I might board?"

"Naeb'dy really comes here tae stay, hen. More of a thoroughfare unless yer wan o' the locals, ye know whit a' mean, hen?" His words bite at her ears with the chill of the North Sea wind.

She tilts her head to try to make sense of his peculiar mumbling. Playing him back and translating it in her mind. She sighs deeply. Her exasperation and exhaustion almost have her in tears. Jenna's bloodshot eyes begin to water.

"Uch, there's nae need tae greet. Once ye get yer bearings, ye'll get somewhere tae stop." He snorted, rubbing his nose on his sleeve. "If ye follow that walkway doon the steps there by the seafront fur aboot ten minutes. Ye'll come tae the pub—The Drouthy Mare. Wee Jeanie Robertson owns the place. She'll sort ye oot wi a hot cuppa and help ye find somewhere for longer. She'll give ye a bed for the night."

"Thanks." Jenna follows the direction of the stranger's finger, walking down a rough road by the harbor. From photos online, Jenna assumed this part of Scotland was mostly gray, with the hills surrounding the low-lying villages and hamlets on all sides blocking most of the good light. Here, though, a whisper of blue plays at the borders of dark drifting clouds, creating unusual shadows of pale greens and blues over the landscape, like spilled water colors. *I wonder if it's always so moody here.*

Pushing her damp hood back from her face, Jenna welcomes the pub's warmth. It's a Friday evening, and groups of families, friends and neighbors are gathered, laughing and filling the stools at the bar. The atmosphere is friendly and inviting. A small open fire is crackling at the opposite wall of the small bar, and a cairn terrier and a border collie are stretched out in front of the hearth. They're clearly used to the bustle of The Drouthy Mare. Though a public place, it has a home-away-from-home feel.

"Could I get a table, please?" The girl collecting glasses gives Jenna the side-eye, taking in her long legs and wild hair. "It's just me. Anything will do. Maybe you could suggest what's good to order too?" Jenna holds out a bill to the girl. Cash is the universal friend-maker, regardless of where in the world one is—popping it between her breasts, the cute blonde winks, nodding in the direction of a small table for two against the wall by the bar.

"Over here. I'm not supposed to tie up a table on Friday nights. It's oor busiest. I'll lay doon an extra place setting so it looks like you're waiting for someone else. Do you like fish? If so, I suggest oor Friday Special—smoked haddock stovies with freshly baked oatcakes. My Da brings tatties from the farm weekly. Oors are the best—everyone loves them, and the dish is obviously locally caught. As I'm sure, ye may have guessed in a wee fishing village."

"I'll order whatever you recommend. But, what's stovies?"

"Ye never had stovies? Uch, then yer in for a treat. Ye'll love it. It's a good hearty tattie— ehh... I mean, *potato-based* dish. It never fails to warm ye up when it's dreich like this. Tonight's is made with our famous smoked haddock. I never used to like fish, but the way it's prepared here is the best."

Jenna snickered. She really was far from home. The way the young woman tried to say potato, with almost an American accent, made her laugh inside.

"Sounds great. I'll have that and a pint of whatever's on tap. Is there a Jeanie I can speak with about a room?"

"She's oot back, checking on an order coming in. I'll point her in yer direction when she's free."

Jenna sets her bag under the table, then runs her fingers through her hair, smoothing it around her shoulders. *I probably look like death on a cracker.*

Despite the travel and weather, the young woman's appeal stands out. She quickly averts her eyes when a couple of men at the bar raise their glasses at her, smiling. *Attention is the last thing I need right now. Food, a hot bath, and rest, then I can think this all through.*

The waitress returns with a pint of nectar-colored ale, "Here ye go, again, it's one of our most popular."

"Looks refreshing. Exactly what I need. Thanks. What is it?"

"It's Fraoch. A popular heather ale, you'll love it. Your food won't be long."

Jenna smiles and takes a sip as the waitress turns and delivers drinks to another table. "Mmm," licking her lips. She'd never tasted anything like it—floral, peaty, the flavor burst in her mouth. It was distinctly refreshing and light, exactly what Jenna needed.

Her meal arrives from the kitchen, steamy and smoky. It was served in a deep, ceramic dish with a side of oatcakes. The food was heaped onto the plate, the aroma was intoxicating, and for a few minutes, Jenna thought of nothing but how delicious the food was. Her stomach rumbled in appreciation as she gobbled it.

"Are you expecting someone? They're crazy to keep you waiting." The male voice behind her is deep and seductive. Jenna panics. *It can't be Layton. There's no fucking way he found me so fast.* She's too shocked to protest when a well-built man wearing a worn blue plaid shirt with the sleeves rolled up slides into the chair opposite her. Reaching for one of the remaining oatcakes on her plate, Jenna notices that his hands are large and clean but also gnarly with scars. There's a red streak near his thick eyebrow in the shape of an arrow, extending down onto his cheekbone that doesn't take away from how handsome he is. Biting into the cracker, his eyes crinkle as she sputters a protest.

"Please. I'm not up to having a conversation, I don't mean to be rude, but I'm tired and want to sleep. Are you laughing at me because I'm not interested? It's rude to plop down assuming I'm interested in sharing my table."

Head down, he reaches up to smooth one side of his black hair. It's pulled back into a messy topknot at the crown, and a small hoop earring catches the light. His beard is short and trimmed close, enhancing his strong jaw. When he looks up, not discouraged by Jenna's snippy response, his clear blue-gray eyes are speckled with green.

He's laughing at her.

"I couldn't help myself. I had trouble breathing when you blew through the door. I'm Grant Sutherland, and I've not seen the likes of you around here before. An American is rare in these parts. A beautiful American woman alone is rarer still. Tell me you're new in town and that you're here to stay?"

"I'm not telling you anything, Sir. Or Grant, or whatever. Go bother one of those cute girls' eye-fucking you at the bar." Jenna's fork clatters to the table. She's flustered. When he reaches over to steady her hand, lightly brushing the tops of her fingers with his thumb, Jenna wants to pull it back or slap him. She does neither because this stranger's raw energy is exciting. This man reminds her of Layton, but there's nothing forbidding about him.

"I don't want a thing from you but a bit of conversation. It's been a long week at the forge, and I'm keen to lighten my mood." He isn't budging, and Jenna feels her cheeks growing hot with annoyance and interest, despite herself. Unzipping the neck of her hoody, careful not to expose anything interesting to this man, Jenna leans closer.

"I don't know what a forge is, and I'm not your therapist." Before she's able to insult him enough to make him leave, two men holding glasses of beer bump into him from the side.

"Oi, Grant. Need a bit of help getting Robbie into the truck. He's been at it most of the afternoon, and someone's about to slap his face or kick him in the balls. I'm parked down the street. Can you lend us an arm to steady him out the back door? If Jeanie sees him, it will be the last time he's welcome here." The shorter of the two men clasps Grant on the shoulder. He nods, pushing the chair back. Jenna can't help but admire how tall he is, easily the largest of the men milling about at the bar.

"Rob's a good friend. I need to help wrangle him home, but promise me you'll stay? I won't be long." Grant is annoyed. This happens too often lately, but Rob has much on his mind this time of year, and Grant's had his back since they were kids.

"I won't promise you a thing. I'm hoping for a room as soon as possible. Enjoy your night."

He sniggers, "So, you're staying the night here too? That's good to know," he winks as he helps his friends out the door.

"Another one, Miss?" The girl who seated her points at Jenna's empty glass. Jenna is anxious, but the alcohol is calming.

"Please. Where's the lady's room? I'll be right back." Jenna hopes that by ignoring Grant, he will leave her alone. The blonde girl nods towards a doorway.

"Just through there, right up the stairs, and it's the door at the top."

DELEVAN HOUSE

"Bring whatever she wants on me, Brianna." Grant's voice booms over the crowd, gravelly and thick. She nods, and with a tray full of empty glasses in the air, she heads to the bar. He's helping the other two men escort their friend, Rob, with early streaks of silver in his hair, to the back of the pub.

Jenna navigates the crowd to the ladies, an odd *place to put the restrooms in a bar—at the top of the stairs.* She wonders if they have many accidents. Walking back to her table is a chore. It's more crowded now. Her feet stick to the floor, she trips, then catches herself, feeling eyes on her. A younger-looking woman is standing in her way, wearing a slip of a green silk dress and a heavily embroidered shawl around her shoulders. Jenna feels even rougher. Her black clothing is sticky from the day. The woman in front of her is classy for a local bar. She has sharp angled cheekbones and cat-like intense chartreuse eyes. Her look is almost alien. Striking. The kind of woman who probably didn't really *belong* anywhere. Jenna understood that. Yet she exuded a presence that no one would dare question. The sharp, sleek cut of her hair added to the divinity of her features.

"You look like you could use a friend. This place is out of control tonight. I'm Caoimhe. May I join you for a pint?"

"Jenna. I'd like that. I'm trying to connect with the owner, Jeanie. The driver who dropped me here said she had rooms to rent. Do you know her?"

"I do." Caoimhe regards Jenna with an intensity she's never experienced from another woman. But she's welcoming of someone who might help, particularly the safety of a woman's company.

"I'll make sure Jeanie knows you require a place. Will you be staying long?" Caoimhe gestures to the barmaid, who scrambles to their end of the worn bar, then leaning in, she whispers a few words.

"Yes, I understand. I'll let her know right away."

"You're all set. Jeanie will make up a room upstairs with fresh sheets for you."

"Thank you so much. I sure appreciate the kindness." Jenna lightly hugs Caoimhe, relieved.

Taking Jenna's hand in hers, Caoimhe glides effortlessly through the crowd. Shockingly, no one glances in her direction, although she's stunning. The women sit back down at Jenna's table, where foamy pints are waiting.

"That was fast." Caoimhe sips, blotting at the corner of her mouth with her shawl. Jenna smiles.

"What brings you here? Few folks pass this way for the heck of it, and you're too pretty to be a lost lamb." Caoimhe's skin is flawless. She has the look of an impossible lean yet curvy couture model. Thick black eyeliner, extending out past the corners of her eyes, is the only makeup she wears. Her impossibly long eyelashes wing out on either side like an exotic cat. A spattering of light freckles spritz across her nose and cheeks.

"Passing through. Someone gave me the wrong address on a B&B rental. I'll try to sort it out after I get some rest. It's been a rough couple of days." Jenna mindlessly fingers the necklace. Her manicured fingers caress the textured silver as if it had been given to her by a long-lost lover. The stone glimmers. It didn't need light to dazzle. *She* was imbued with her own light. Caoimhe longed to have it and considered there was more to her longing than helping her mother. She smiles warmly at the stranger.

"Boy trouble. I know of it well. Did he give you that fabulous piece of jewelry? I noticed it right away when you walked by." Jenna glances down. Somehow, the necklace feels heavier than before on her neck, almost too heavy. *I'm just tired.*

"Kind of. It's a long story. We're not together anymore."

"Well, it's gorgeous. Would you consider selling it to me? I don't mean to be rude. I collect rare pieces such as yours and would love to have it. You can name your price. I promise I won't be offended." Jenna rubs her fingers over the green stone. It feels hot to the touch.

"I'm not sure. Maybe. I don't know if I want to hang onto it much longer—memories and all." Jenna considers passing the necklace on. It won't be her problem anymore if Layton sends someone looking for it. And her.

"Well, let's enjoy our drinks. You sleep on it. I'll be around for a day or so and would love to see you again. Do you have plans in the area? It will be fun to show you around if you're free." Something about Caoimhe makes Jenna feel like she can trust her. She's confident and calm and reminds Jenna of herself. That is when she's not running for her life. She reminds Jenna of the woman she wants to be.

"Damn. He's back." Jenna flushes red averting her eyes to the bar, where Grant is surveying the room. "Do you know him? That guy was annoying me earlier."

The graceful girl turns slightly, glancing in the same direction. Smoothing her wrap, Caoimhe eases back in her chair, stretching out comfortably. She crosses her ankles, lazily eying the man up and down.

"I believe I know of him. He's a blacksmith from the next village over. I'm not interested in him tonight, though." Her voice is a soft purr under the noise of the pub. Taken aback slightly, Jenna raises an eyebrow. *Is she flirting with me?*

"I hope you don't think I'm available?"

"Not interested in you in that way either. I have work to do and no time for any amusements. I need to leave, but I'll come by early tomorrow afternoon if you have no plans. Maybe you'd like to spend a couple of days in the nearby village with me. They'll have a special celebration soon that only happens once every several years. A real treat for a tourist." Caoimhe continues eying Jenna's necklace intently, then smiles. Her gaze is direct and predatory, but Jenna is alone, scared, and vulnerable. And she's always been drawn to predators.

"That sounds great. I'm going to finish this one, then head upstairs. He seems to have found someone else to bother. He's definitely not my type. I'm staying clear of all men for the foreseeable future." Grant's engaged in deep conversation with another man, clutching the hand of a girl who looks drunk. Jenna takes this as a sign to remove herself from his line of sight.

Caoimhe kisses her new friend lightly on the cheek—her perfume is musky and strong. With a swish of her fancy shawl, she's gone. Jenna tosses back the rest of her beer, then gathers her things to head upstairs. The blonde is cleaning a table as Jenna, trying to be casual in her departure, leaves the rowdy crowd behind. She directs her to a narrow staircase off to the side of the entrance.

DELEVAN HOUSE

"Up there, Miss. Second door on the right. It's open, so just throw the bolt for privacy when you're inside the room, and I wish you a good night."

Jenna presses a bill into the girl's hand, then climbs the steep steps. The upper floor smells earthy and hoppy, with an overlay of furniture polish. The small room is simply furnished and decorated. Hung on the walls are a few oil paintings of highland cows and sheep. They look dated, but the linens are fresh, and the fixtures sparkle in the tiny bathroom when she turns on the lamp by the bed. It's quiet and calm. *This is the most beautiful room I've ever seen.*

As soon as she sits down, every muscle in the young woman's body collapses. Her body is screaming with fatigue. *I need a hot bath first.* The cast iron claw-foot tub is chipped around the edges, but there are thick white towels neatly folded on the floor. The taps scream when Jenna turns them on, but steam fills the room within minutes.

I need to find some decent clothes tomorrow. Jenna has no intention of ever wearing the cheap black traveling ensemble again and kicks the clothing to one side as she slides into the soothing water.

Fingering the necklace, she wonders if Layton will come for her and decides not to risk having the piece if he does. *I'll sell it to Caoimhe. I'll need all the cash I can get until I figure out what my future looks like.*

Jenna closes her eyes and dozes as the soft water washes away dirt and stress. The water gently sloshes, covering her weary body, up to her chin. There's a hearty knock on the door, startling her peace. "Fuck!" She jerks up, and water spills over the side of the tub, soaking the tiled floor. *Who'd bother me? It's probably the owner wondering if the room is okay.*

Bundling a towel around her, she remembers she has nothing clean to wear. *I'm not putting those filthy things back on. I'll just crack the door enough to look out.*

There's another knock.

The heavy bolt doesn't slide easily. When she pulls it harder in frustration, Jenna scrambles to keep the damp towel wrapped around her as she inches it open the smallest possible crack.

He's standing there, Grant Sutherland. He's even taller than she remembered from earlier, with an amused smirk. His eyes drift over her, and she suddenly feels more exposed than she is. This stranger's lust rolls from him, and she feels intoxicated by the idea of his skin all over hers. *Perhaps, this is what I need to wash Layton away.*

"All you have to do is say one word. No." Running his hand through his ridiculously sexy hair with a practiced gesture, Grant smiles. His eyes are intense, pupils wide and wanting. He bites his lower lip, and Jenna has never felt anything as intense as this man's lust for her. "But you won't."

He's right. She won't refuse him.

She opens the door wide, her consent and intent as clear as his. She drops the towel.

The cool air brushes her skin, and her areolas tighten, puckering her brown-pink nipples. Her skin tingles—goosebumps. She shivers, not from the cold. She's physically reacting to this man before he has even laid a finger on her.

DELEVAN HOUSE

Grant enters the room and slams the door at his back. He doesn't bother to lock it. He doesn't care. He has one thing on his mind, written all over him as his eyes drink in her body.

Jenna pictures him wrapping his muscular arms around her waist and throwing her on the bed. And driving into her. She can't stop quivering as he just stands there with his eyes all over her. He removes his heavy work boots, undoing the laces and tossing them to the side of the door without once taking his eyes off her body.

"Oh, girl, you're in for it now," he growls. His voice is husky with desire. His accent is thick. Her pussy throbs and she hopes it doesn't show on her face. She was already on display.

He drops to his knees in front of Jenna, picks up the fluffy white towel pooled around her dainty feet, and tosses it to the side. He draws his hands from her ankles up her legs, cups her buttocks with his large, strong, rough hands, and stares at her sex.

She parts her legs a little, so he can get a better look at her.

"My god..." he growls again and slowly lifts his gaze from her neat mound to her eyes.

"You...

are...

fucking...

beautiful," he emphasizes each word, drawing each out in a thick Scots drawl—rugged, wild, confident. The accent makes him sound even more masculine somehow. Jenna had never wanted a man more than at this moment.

From the man that appeared at her door, she assumed he was slightly drunk to be so forthwith. He was utterly sober now, but it was clear that he fully intended on getting intoxicated with her.

Jenna swallows hard. Her mouth is dry, and her pussy is wet. She could not think of ever wanting someone more than this beast on his knees before her.

He tightens his grip around her buttocks, tearing his eyes from hers. He nuzzles his face into her sex, inhales her scent, and she feels his growls against her lips as he begins kissing her there. He sucks hard at her soft, delicate folds, causing her body to pull away, raising up on her tiptoes like a goddess elevated by his worship. Except she couldn't pull away. His huge hands are clamped on her ass, and he keeps her firmly on his face.

Softening his mouth, he loosens his grip slightly, though not enough for Jenna to move, and licks her rhythmically. Running his thick, wet tongue the length of her opening, back and forth, back and forth. Her eyelids flicker. She relinquishes any control and gives over willingly. To this man. In this room. In this odd little village.

"Mmmm...." he grumbles his delight into her. Jenna's head swims, and for the first time, she's not thinking about running. She's not thinking about Layton. She doesn't care about anything but the tingling that this beautiful man is creating between her legs.

Tension marches up her calves, and she moves her pelvis back and forth, along with Grant's sensational tongue. She grinds herself into it, riding his face. Her movement causes him to groan in hunger against her.

Fuck. Fuck. Fuck. Jenna hisses, biting back her words. *I wasn't going to do this. Maybe this is the first thing that's gone*

DELEVAN HOUSE

right since I departed that damn plane. Fuck it. I need this. She lets her mind be clouded over with the demands of the flesh.

Panting, her breasts rise and fall with electricity building in her center. Her eyes flutter, and she throws her head back as she rides this stranger's face harder. His tongue plunges inside her, and his nails bite her skin—*bloody hell.*

Jenna had never come from oral alone before; she didn't think she could. She wants to scream. Her panting speeds and his noises become more animal-like.

Jenna's skin grows clammy. She looks down again at this head between her legs and threads her fingers into his hair. She grinds harder, not caring if she suffocates him with her need. Tunnel vision takes over. And she, too, begins grunting as she rides his face and hungry tongue faster as demanded by the heat building through her central nervous system.

The fuse was about to blow.

Jenna moans, low and light. She emanates sounds more guttural—primal. That incredible energy morphs within her, twisting into an unstoppable vortex and gushes out.

The rising continues within her. Heat gallops the length of her spine and radiates through the base of her skull as she rocks her pelvis against this man's face. His lips and his tongue consume her.

The tension was now building in her head, hot and almost unbearable. Part of her body wanted to pull away. She felt she may combust. Even if she could, his vice-grip wouldn't have let her go. And if she could, there is no way her legs would hold.

It hit.

NATASHA SINCLAIR AND RUTHANN JAGGE

The explosion that was building like a rising tsunami inside her rushed through her, and she cried her orgasm into the world. His tongue drove into her faster as she screamed.

Her orgasm ebbs slowly from her body. Her heart is banging in her head. Jenna tries to learn to breathe again and wills herself back into her body from the transcendent orgasm. She finds her vision returning from the sparks of ecstasy that had shattered her. Jenna blinks down at the man between her soaking thighs.

Grant stands up. He glides his hands up her body and steers her back towards the bed. He has to; her legs are jelly. The look in his eyes tells her he knows his talent. He lays her back. Then wipes his mouth with the sleeve of his plaid shirt. She cracks her neck and stretches out, looking a little spent.

"Wow, there, lassie. Don't get any ideas. I am not done with you yet." Grant towers over the bed. His hair is messy from her tugging at it. He looks even sexier than he had before. Unbuttoning his shirt, the look in his eyes is pure sex. And Jenna was far from done with him either. She moves towards him, crawls down the bed, and undoes his jeans. It's her turn to show him what she can do with her mouth.

Jenna wakes in a tangle of sheets. The thick blankets are strewn on the floor. The unsettling feeling of not knowing where she was skittered over her bare skin. Layton always expected her to be on call by 8 am, looking her best and prepared for his worst. Waking with no alarm was foreign. Her entire body ached in the most wonderful way. Every muscle had been stretched out like never before. Her pussy throbbed. She smiled lazily, then realized she was alone in the room. Anger flared in her as she sat up. On the bedside table, a note was scrawled:

I'm sorry I got you all dirty after your bath. Perhaps I'll join you for the clean-up next time. If you're still around, I might catch you tonight when I finish up work.

PS. Apologise to Jeanie for the noise. We weren't quiet!
G X

Jenna rolls her eyes. She pulls a thick blanket from the floor, covers herself, and falls back asleep. She sure needed it.

Sleepily glancing at the old wall clock an hour later, Jenna remembers she has something to get up for. Though she's not sure about her new friend, there is something about Caoimhe that is different. She intrigued Jenna, not just her exotic look. Her presence was almost enthralling. *She'll be here soon. I've got nowhere and no one else at this point; let's see how the day goes.*

Getting out of the creaky (now creakier) bed, she quickly gets dressed. Pulling on the same weary clothing she's been wearing for two days disgusts her, but until she finds replacements, they'll have to do.

Pulling her hair back, Jenna fingers the green stone still clasped around her neck. *Maybe I should hold on to this for a while.* Her luck seems to be changing since she put it on.

"Are you ready for a bit of the wild side of this forsaken place?" Caoimhe is leaning against a polished black car. Sleek and sophisticated, she's a striking contrast to the gray mist of the sky above and the few villagers walking the street in front of the pub.

"Thank you for the hospitality." The door bangs behind Jenna. She went to the kitchen for tea and toast, but it was empty, with no provisions to be found. No one seemed to be around at all. The place seemed to have died with the daylight. "I'm glad to see you, but I'm hungry and need something hot with caffeine to get me started." Caoimhe laughs, opening the passenger door.

Bloody hell. She smells divine. Jenna is awash by the surprising fragrance of her new guide flowing out into the chill. Her eyes flutter involuntarily as she inhales the notes of sandalwood and warm, inviting vanilla radiating from the woman, riding above the salty sea air.

"We'll get you sorted out. There's a bakery not far. The Granary has the best of it all—sweet and savory." Side-eying her ride, Jenna is more disgusted at her own appearance. Caoimhe is dressed in perfectly fitting black pants, with high-laced boots and a soft green sweater. Her signature shawl with the white bird embroidery draped over one shoulder, then cinched at the waist with a wide studded black leather belt. Her winged eyeliner is perfect on both sides, something Jenna has never been able to master. *She looks like a fucking gothic runway model.*

As they fasten up in the car, the engine gently purrs as Caoimhe pulls out. "Is there somewhere I can pick up something fresh to wear? I am a fright and definitely not dressed for this chill."

"Not to worry. We're similar in size, and I'm due for a closet purge. We'll stop at my cottage before we head out on an adventure, and I'm sure you'll find something that suits you."

DELEVAN HOUSE

Her unexpected kindness touches Jenna. It's been a while since anyone bothered with her needs.

"Sounds great, are you sure? I can pick something up unless you're getting rid of some things."

"Positive. We'll leave my car at the dock and ferry over. You'll like Macha, it's quiet, and there's no one to judge what you're wearing or not wearing." Caoimhe winks. "The water will be calm this early in the day."

"Ferry? You don't live here?"

"Macha is a little bit offshore. I prefer privacy." Caoimhe points to a dark piece of land a distance from shore. Jenna squints to see the land through the low cloud and smirry rain. Caoimhe parks in an open lot near the docks. Everything stinks of fish and salty sea air, and the men loading up the boats for a day's work look miserable.

Jenna nods. *What have I gotten myself into?*

A small green and white weather-battered passenger ferry bobs against the dock, and Caoimhe waves to the man tying off the line. It's the same craggy local who first greeted Jenna when she arrived. The man with three fingers. Frowning, his face a wrinkled mass of annoyance, he waves the women down.

"I see ye found an escort." He's staring at Jenna, mumbling in Caoimhe's direction, but not making eye contact with the beauty."

"Yes. Hello again. We met at the pub." Jenna smiles uncomfortably.

Holding Jenna's hand, he steadies her as she steps onto the boat. Caoimhe expertly steps up and slides into place on the bench with no assistance.

"Over to Macha as fast as you can. No side trips. We have things to do." He nods but doesn't say anything else as he cranks the boat to life.

Jenna's not keen on watercraft, but smiles as Caoimhe clicks the lock on the bold orange lifejacket into place, then takes her hand. Narrowing her eyes, Caoimhe watches as Jenna clutches the jewel around her neck, its heavy silver chain sparking in the light. *I wonder if she feels the allure of the noose she clutches.* Caoimhe pictures the painting hung over her mother's mantel. Her mother, back when she was so beautiful that everyone would fall at her feet. And many feared what they could do if she willed them to do so. The painting in her memory was of her mother sitting on the chair made for her by Laird Delevan. With wood lovingly felled from Badb Wood, carved by his own hands in adoration of his wife, and upholstered in luxurious flocked velvet emerald fabric by the best seamstress in the village. Fraoch perched on her left shoulder, looking fierce and protective. Her mother's fingers softly rested on *her* necklace—one of a kind like its owner. It could have been a third eye; the pendant exuded its own soul. Caoimhe tears her eyes from the pendant and forces a smile turning up her mouth towards the pretty stranger. A trusting smile is returned.

The motor is noisy and sputtering. There's no conversation as they bounce over to Macha. Jenna notices thick clusters of birds in the sky above. They look like dense black smoke. When she points to them, Caoimhe nods dismissively. It's a brief and not too rough ride over the waves to the small island, thick with trees and a pebbled beach.

DELEVAN HOUSE

Unclicking the lifejackets, "That's us here. Are you okay? You look a little green around the gills?"

"I'll be alright. I wasn't expecting to have my feet off land." Jenna swallows back, her mouth suddenly dry.

Caoimhe softly laughs, "Ahhh, my girl, adventure keeps us fresh!"

"When are ye wanting a return, Miss?" the man asks. He's anxious to leave. His eyes are on the mainland when he speaks.

Jenna was glad to be on land again, even though the boat ride was uneventful; the choppy water was a trial on her unaccustomed sea legs. She arches her head back, breathing in the salt air, then remembering her manners, fumbles in her bag. She holds out a few bills to the man.

"I'm sorry, I have no idea if this is enough. Do you need more?" Caoimhe raises her hand to stop her, then pushes the bills back into Jenna's hand. Her pointed nails are sharp and painted a brilliant shade of red.

"Tomorrow at the same time," Caoimhe says, pointing her eyebrows. He nods, shoving off back into the sea. Not looking back, the boat speeds off.

"My place is right around the bend, a five-minute walk." Ignoring Jenna's concern for the boatman, Caoimhe heads down a path formed of the same pebbles of the beach, ignoring the damage to the high heels of her expensive boots. She still manages to look graceful. Even in her sensible shoes, Jenna stumbles to keep up with her new friend, gliding up the stone path as if it were a polished catwalk runway. "I've got some delicious tea, and we'll rest a minute. Then you can raid my closet."

Excited, Jenna manages to match her pace. There's a small cottage ahead. The garden in front is overgrown, but not with weeds and brambles. Trellised plants and trees lush with red berries line the path. There's an ornate, heavy carved wooden gate at the entrance.

"It's pretty—I love the trees with the berries. Can you eat them?" Jenna reaches up, plucking a cluster, then breathes in the scent. Caoimhe slaps it out of her hand, crushing the berries under her foot.

"No, absolutely not when they're ripe and raw. Some cook them into a jelly, but I keep the trees for protection. This island is old, and sometimes, things we bury need reminders to stay that way. The Rowan keeps such things at rest." Jenna shivers. Her hoody is damp from the sea air. Caoimhe slides a key into the lock.

Sparsely but elegantly furnished, Jenna notices the beautiful antiques in the room as soon as the door opens. A fireplace with cordwood wood is neatly stacked and ready for a fire. Caoimhe gestures Jenna down a narrow hallway.

"This way. I have a girlfriend who looks after the place for me, so it's kept clean and well-stocked. It's small but cozy. I don't spend much time here; I'm too much of a prowler. Make yourself comfortable." There's a fancy quilt on the four-poster bed in the guestroom. Sliding her hand over the smooth fabric, Jenna notices the tiny, precise hand-stitching.

"This is exceptional. You don't see handwork like this often anymore."

"Yes, it was made by a woman from the island where I was born. Minerva Morvin is a mistress of the needle, and she made it for me years ago. We'll go there for a visit tomorrow. Why don't you take a minute? I need to check on a few things. Then we can have some tea and get you kitted out." She moves like a trained dancer floating on air, and Jenna feels more awkward than usual when she's with this woman.

"The bathroom?" Jenna asks.

"Of course. It's just down there to the left. Help yourself to anything you need."

There's a soft white robe hanging on a hook inside the bathroom door, so Jenna splashes some water on her face, drops her clothing on the floor, and then snuggles into the thick cotton. Jenna heads back down the hall, admiring the view of the choppy blue sea from the window. "I'm here." Caoimhe's tossing garments onto a green velvet duvet. Her room is large, with dark wood furnishings and heavy silk drapes. The dramatic effect seems out of place for a sea cottage but matches the owner perfectly. "Grab a few things and see what you think?" Jenna picks up a knit dress, then a pair of black trousers, blinking hard at the labels. *Everything piled on this bed is high couture!* She knows the names from her days with Layton.

"Are you sure? These are really nice pieces. Not exactly throwaway?"

"Take whatever you want. They're just clothes, right." Caoimhe selects a red sweater, a tailored jacket, and a sexy leather skirt. "Try these on. I know they'll be great on you. I'm going to make tea while you play." Bundling the clothing into Jenna's arms, she's gone again, like a ghost.

Everything Jenna puts on fits perfectly, right down to a pair of chunky ankle boots, similar to a favorite pair she left behind. Folding a few items neatly, she changes back into the oversized robe.

"I don't know what to say. Thank you! Is there anything I can do to repay you?" Jenna joins Caoimhe standing at the porthole window in the small kitchen, wearing the same robe, looking out at the sea while sipping a cup of tea.

"I don't often have company, and I'm glad you can use them. Nothing comes to mind. Except I'll ask again if you'll consider selling me your necklace. I don't keep valuables here, but we'll visit Badb tomorrow. I keep a box of special things my mother gave me locked in a vault there. You'll see why I'm interested in adding it to my collection."

Jenna's grown used to the substantial gem hanging around her neck. She hasn't taken it off since finding it in Layton's office. *I wonder if he's looking for it.* She decides to be honest with her new friend.

"I'm going to hang onto it for a while. It belonged to someone I thought cared for me. To be honest, I took it from him, and I'm afraid he may send someone to find it, and I don't want to involve you. Obviously, it has value, if not monetary. I hope you'll understand." She's clutching the piece, feeling the strange vibration against her hand again.

"I do. No pressure. I've learned to ask for what I want. I think you'll like this blend. Try the tea, my girl Elspeth selects the herbs from the garden, and it's delicious." She's holding out a blue enamel mug flecked with white. Jenna sips, nodding in agreement.

Changing the subject, Caoimhe cups her hands around hers. The rising steam gives her a distinctly inhuman look. "Let's sit. You can tell me all about him." Picking up a plate of sandwiches and shortbread, she heads to the fireplace, where logs are spitting flames. The two young women curl up in front of the fire like old friends, snacking and sipping. For an hour, Jenna gets the situation regarding Layton off her mind, sharing intimate details and concerns. There's something about Caoimhe that makes her feel it's okay when she reaches over with a linen napkin to dab at the tears on Jenna's cheeks.

"I think you're incredibly brave. Believe me. I know all about how deceiving relationships can be. I've only had one true love since we were young, but he wants nothing to do with me now that we are free to enjoy each other completely. He's too afraid of what others think." She lies to keep camaraderie with the girl-talk and comfort the girl.

"Does he live nearby?" Jenna is enjoying the conversation.

"No, in the village we're going to tomorrow. You talked to him last night in the Drouthy Mare. We have a complicated history, to say the least."

Jenna picks at her fingernail. *Grant. She's talking about Grant.*

"Yeah, he's nothing special, no big loss." *He's an absolute dream of a lover, and I'd die to have him again.*

"I enjoy batting my lovers around like a ball of yarn. His day is coming." Caoimhe winks, but her face is a confusing mix of love and hate. Jenna squirms, standing up from the plush-flowered couch they are sharing. *It's best I don't say another word.*

"Forgive me. The fatigue is hitting hard." Caoimhe nods, gathering the leftovers.

"Rest well. I'm a night owl. If you need anything, I'll probably be up reading. We'll head back to pick up the car tomorrow, and then I'll give you a tour of my hunting grounds. We get some big beasties out here. Don't fret, though. You're safe here. Just lock your door—there's a deadbolt. We can never be too careful, and I want you to rest easy."

"Big beasties?" she says, "Is it not just the mythical haggis you have running amok here?" Jenna jokes.

Caoimhe gives a courtesy laugh. "If only all our monsters were myths," she replies light-heartedly.

Jenna smiles warmly, "Thanks again for a nice day and the lovely clothing. Rest well. I'm looking forward to it." Jenna's head barely hits the pillow before she's asleep.

The cottage is quiet, with only the sound of the murmuring sea outside.

Elspeth, who normally keeps the house, is on the mainland, leaving Caoimhe to tidy up after her guest. Ever the attentive hostess. She gathers the dirty clothing from the bathroom floor. Having practiced subduing her heightened senses, and now home and alone with the guest safely in bed behind the locked door, she lets her guard down... *Grant.*

The musky metallic aroma of *her* Grant arouses her senses. His scent dissolves in her saliva and floods her nostrils and her mind. She was swimming in his aroma, his masculine musk. She could smell his need all over the garments. Her body reacted in jolts. Her mind drowning in his scent, like falling into the pools of his eyes for the first time. His musk was intense and sexual, and then the other scents hit her, intermingled with *her* man. Caoimhe smells, no, she tastes the sex of her guest. She licks the air and flares her nostrils, disgusted but *needing* to gather all she can. The story caught in the fibers of this *other woman's* clothing. *They had been together. She could see it, feel them together. Her Grant inside of this other woman. This foreigner. This damn yank. How dare she come here and take what doesn't belong to her.* Her heart races, the pulse in her neck quickens, and she wants to tear something apart. Jenna. She wants to tear Jenna apart. *He is mine.*

...
...

Jenna was too heavy in sleep to hear what clawed at her door during the night. The thing that was so feverishly baying for her blood.

Caoimhe has a steaming pot of tea and toast slathered in lemon curd set out when Jenna makes her way into the kitchen. Since she arrived, the food tastes amazing, and she's quick to grab a slice. It's as if she had been numbed, and suddenly, she was becoming alive again.

"Hope you rested well. The wind was especially noisy last night."

"I did, for the most part, but is it normal for it to sound like a woman screaming?"

Caoimhe sips, then winces, blowing on her tea to cool it. *Damn. My frayed nerves are showing.*

"Maybe it was a Banshee," she jests. "Why don't you get ready? Our ride back to my car will be here soon. Throw on something cute and grab a jacket. We'll head over to Badb, my home village. It's quiet there, for the most part. You'll have a chance to rest and maybe make some life choices." *And I'll have a chance to make a few decisions as well.*

"Sounds good. Not looking forward to the creepy guy with the boat, but okay, see you in a few."

Jenna saunters down the hall. The weight of the last few days on her shoulders is lessening. She's eager to figure out her next move. *Maybe a remote village will suit me for a while.* She needs somewhere she can be herself again. Dressing in the stylish outfit she tried on last night, she knots her hair back into a ponytail with a scarf, dabs on makeup from her bag, and folds a few chic clothes into her tote bag, regretfully leaving the majority behind. Tucking the necklace with the green stone inside her sweater, she blows herself a farewell kiss in the mirror. *I'm back to being the girl with nothing, but at least I'm wiser.*

Caoimhe's in the front garden, deep in conversation with an intense-looking young woman. "This is Jenna. Jenna, my friend Elspeth." Caoimhe's introduction is perfunctory. Elspeth nods dismissively at Jenna, then squeezes her friend's arm before briskly walking away in silence. A few black birds circle low above her head, and she waves them off as if annoyed by their boldness.

"She seems nice." Jenna rolls her eyes, then catches herself. She's dependent on her new friend for the time being and doesn't want to seem ungrateful. Caoimhe is oblivious to her attitude. It's cooler today, and the leaves of the trees look three-dimensional as they shudder.

"All set? Good, I'm anxious to have some fun." Caoimhe's embroidered shawl flutters out on either side like wings in the sharp breeze, but she's oblivious in her green silk dress. Leaning back with her arms extended, she looks up at the shifting sky. Jenna follows her peculiar new friend's gaze skyward. She's not sure if it's a deeper shade of green because of a reflection from the brilliant silk or if it's an anomaly that's normal in this part of the world.

"Might rain, but we'll be high and dry by then. The moon's got a strong pull on these waters, and it's almost full."

"Is it usually so... vibrant? I mean, I don't think I've ever seen the sky that color?" Jenna asks.

"Oh. It's quite something. She likes to put on a show does our aurora, and this is just a glimmer of her magick. A tease of what's soon to come." Caoimhe winks, but the playful action doesn't break the intensity stretched across her face. She somehow looked less friendly than she had yesterday. Her features are sharper, and she looks hungry.

"Aurora? Like the famous princess?"

Caoimhe chuckles softly, "No, this one is far older than that. The aurora borealis is the magicks you'll see dance across the sky, Na Fir Chlis, the merry dancers, the northern lights. People come from all over the world to try to catch a glimpse. You'll see them in their boats with their lenses, hoping for a clear night to witness the enigmatic spectacle."

"Is it always like this, then? What causes it?"

"Not always. When Beira dominates the wheel, the dancers command the show."

"I'm sorry, I feel so ignorant... Beira?"

"Winter, darling, Beira is the Goddess of Winter. She is perhaps the fiercest of all our deities. The laminations can be witnessed when there are no snowy blizzards and her fury is in that chilly stasis. For those who take the time to look up. A phenomenon that seems almost ancient when in the more populated areas. Then, perhaps that's why the magicks are harder to see. When folk choose to be blind to her." Caoimhe watches the stranger as she ponders her words. Then continued, "Scientists say that the images painted by the merry dancers in the north are mirrored in the south, in the aurora australis. How they can analyze two places at once in the detail that explodes in her heights of ambers, greens, blues and yellows, I don't understand. Humans like to claim answers for just about everything these days. Always looking inward or down, and often missing the point." Caoimhe continued intensely regarding Jenna.

Jenna didn't know what to say. She didn't really understand and fought not to squirm under the intensity of her new *friend's* eyes. She only asked about the color of the sky, wondering if it warned of a storm. *Am I missing something?* She felt a little out of her depth.

"Let's go." Caoimhe smiled and ushered her to follow as they headed back toward the beach.

He's waiting at the water's edge, with a knit scarf wrapped tightly around his neck and covering the lower half of his face, mumbling a greeting. The boat seems smaller when the women squeeze in. There's more of a chop in the sea today, and Jenna's stomach is uneasy when he holds out a callused hand to help her when they reach the docks on the other side.

"Watch yerself, Missy. There's deep water all around, and I'm sensing ye don't swim well." His blue eyes are glassy with cataracts. "Stay afloat. This one will pull ye under." Jenna strains to hear his whisper, but Caoimhe is already heading down the dock, car keys jingling in her hand, and she scrambles to catch up.

DELEVAN HOUSE

The black car is covered with a light layer of frost, and Jenna shivers as they slide into the front seat.

"You'll get used to it. This time of the year can be dull. I'm glad you grabbed the Barbour. It's a good jacket. You need to put it on while I warm up the temp in here." Jenna buttons the collar of the stylish, rugged coat tight around her neck. The waxy cotton feels wonderful around her.

"It looks amazing on you!"

"Thank you. Aren't you cold?" Caoimhe's ivory skin shows no sign of redness or dryness, whereas Jenna's nose is running, and she can feel the tiny lines on her face deepening.

"It doesn't bother me. My genetics are unique. I'm a different breed of cat." Caoimhe winks, shifting the car into gear.

Appellation of Fae and Lady

The young woman's grave lay unmarked and undisturbed since the day she was interred in 1424. She was dressed in a simple green smock that covered her body to the ankles, and the noose she used to hang herself, was tucked by her side. The village's embarrassment. No church would allow her to rest in consecrated land.

The shame of this girl who fell in love and spread her legs for a brawny young man was profound.

She stood on the shore with new life budding in her young belly, abandoned by her whaler for his call to the sea. The sin of an unwed whore was sin enough. Then the sin of this same young woman who tried and failed to take her own life was unforgivable.

This young woman was choking on the ocean, her love's one true mistress when a fisherman dragged her from the waves. The stranger forced the water from her lungs, *saving her*. To what end?

She was disowned by her family. Her name was wiped from their lips. And the young woman was condemned to isolation on the outskirts of the population.

She succeeded on her second attempt, thanks to the merciful cooperation of the noose around her dainty neck. Death would be her only peace from pointed fingers and obscene gestures, from the scorn of women clutching their

DELEVAN HOUSE

husbands' hands when she walked by. They could have tried her as a witch as punishment for her sins only a hundred years later.

The forgotten grave was first discovered by peat diggers cutting valuable fuel from the land for the village's crofters in 1574. 150-years after her interment. They respectfully re-covered the coffin with fresh earth. As the grave was clearly disturbed, it was later found again by soldiers. These men exhumed the scarred wooden coffin, looking for gold to steal. What lay inside was not bones and ash as expected but an unearthly beauty.

The body of a young woman who could have been Frejya with a flawless ivory complexion. She was like a porcelain doll. Delicate features appeared to be carved from alabaster, accented by a dimpling of freckles across her nose and cheeks. Her lips were pale but still held a pink blush and the plumpness of youth. She was astoundingly beautiful. Her long, dark auburn hair was thick and lush—impossible to believe, considering the state of the vessel holding her. Men dubbed this as a diabolical, ungodly defiance of nature and re-covered The Lady of Badb for fear of what disturbing this buried angel could mean.

However, some of those men and those who heard the stories of this beauty were singularly drawn to her with a morbid fascination. They mingled their intrigue and fascination with desire and lust. This strange discovery of a perfect female lying in her box and frozen in time lured soldiers back to her spot over and over, repeatedly digging her up to marvel.

A few, void of honor or respect, went further.

There was a beauty who couldn't say no to their sordid desires. Her preserved body began to deteriorate for the first time since she died over one hundred and fifty years earlier. Her decay did not stop these despicable suitors from corroding and defiling her with their salty sweat and fluids.

Her body lay silent, but the torture of men scratched at her beauty and peace.

The torment of the girl's body eventually ripped through her condemned soul, and endless cries of suffering resonated from somewhere between life and death. Her wailing tore apart ancient worlds, crashing through hidden realms. The earth itself heard her screams, rising up to answer her desperate appeal for mercy.

Sinewy roots slivered up from the bogland, piercing through the heathers beneath The Lady as she was repeatedly molested by another lust-crazed fiend. The growths tore through her delicate blackening skin like worn paper, wrapping around her fragile spine. Energy sparked deep in the earth's core and tore sacred ley lines apart in response to her pleas. Skinny vines cracked through seeds and the shells of insects. Those vines spindled around the core of her skeleton, then fused with thick strands and laced up to her brain stem. Energy surged through her deteriorating corpse as the abhorrent soldier, with his filthy pants around his ankles, grunted atop her jerking body, taking her hard against the ground as if she were a mute toy for his amusement.

DELEVAN HOUSE

As the powerful roots took hold, replacing her veins, the deterioration of the Lady of Badb began to recede. Her sunken body swelled, and sinewy muscles reformed. Her long-dead heart stirred in her chest and her organs filled with blood.

The soldier, lost in lust, did not notice the changes as he rutted in the abandoned open. Her damaged skin healed, and the black rot staining her flesh melted away. The Lady was fair and perfect once again. Her body instinctively reacted to the unwanted invasion. Her vaginal muscles clenched, and the soldier groaned with his eyes closed and neck arching towards the sky. He was out of his mind in ecstasy, unaware that the sleeping beauty was awakening.

Fingers stretched, then her wrists, elbows, and biceps moved. Pale arms reached toward the oblivious young Sargent, and she gripped him by the neck. He gasped in horror when her eyelids flew open to empty sockets. The dead girl lunged, pulling his head in close. He gagged on the sourness of her. Her fingernails were ten razors piercing his neck as she pulled him in tighter, forcing his blood to flow down her arms.

The Lady of Badb plunged her face into his wounds—an insatiable lover. She was starved and had one intention—to drain him completely.

Her captivating face was painted in blood as she sucked at the hot metallic liquid, sweet with adrenaline. Her teeth were weak, so she clawed and gouged his flesh open with her fingers, burrowing deep into the gaping wounds.

His shrill screams attracted an obsidian cloud of wings. The sky blackened with corvids, and their hoarse rattles, clicks and caws echoed his screams until they were no more.

Silence.

She threw him to the ground, then straddled the dead man. The Lady eviscerated his belly with her talons, and the heat from his innards collided with the cold air, mingling with the incoming fog.

Covered in gore, she chewed on his organs, forcing their strength into her dry, desperate throat. A voracious thirst demanded it. Her body craved blood, and the only way to stop the searing pain racking her body was more of it. More. Blood will make her whole again. She *needed* all of it inside her desiccated corpse.

When the soldier was drained, The Lady of Badb collapsed onto the peaty moss surrounded by glossy viscera. She slept there on the spongy soil, winds sweeping over her body pulsing with the soul of the mangled soldier.

She did not breathe, but the wind became her lungs. The Lady was resurrected from the sins of the community who had shunned and abandoned her in an unmarked grave. And from those despicable soldiers.

Her life flickered in a series of lonely blinks and her terrible death. Finally, the comfort of being enveloped in the soft earth. It became the mother—not the one of the flesh who abandoned her in disgust—the earth became her true mother. It held her close, and she knew peace.

Until the soldiers. She saw the face of every man who defiled her body, rutting as friends watched, then took a turn, or those who visited her in secret. Every line and scar on their faces bore an impression into her memory. She could taste the beads of sweat that fell onto her dead skin. The Lady of Badb would taste more.

DELEVAN HOUSE

She vowed revenge on those who took from her without permission or guilt.

She manifested energy from her fury. The Lady's eyes shot open. The September moon rose in a clear sky, blinking with dead rocks, proving how mesmerizing the dead can be. Her supple flesh glowed in its light. Crunching and slurping noises caught her attention as she rested under a blanket of stars. Carrion birds were consuming what remained of the soldier. Innards glistened in their hungry beaks, reflecting in their beady eyes. Their frenzied feeding was as ravenous as she felt. Her phantom eyes were only capable of registering shapes and heat signatures of pumping blood. The Lady of Badb's lids closed. She slumbered, surrounded by the feasting birds.

Time passed, with the shifting of clouds and distant flutter of wings. For one so long dead, the concept of time was ambiguous. The living put too much stock into it and wasted what they had of the slippery sand.

The night air thickened into a heavy oil paint sludge, pressing upon The Lady's bloodied limbs. A cascade of inky feathers churned above in slow-motion—an ebony tornado. There was no sound to accompany the movement in the windless air. Then a whisper broke the silence, like a voice penetrating a dream from another dimension.

Thousands of voices floated from the vortex of feathers. The Lady's eyes opened again; milky marbles. And the birds cawed and screeched towards the North Sea.

A thunderous crack rocked the earth.

The sky flashed and glowed with every conceivable shade of blue: azure, cyan, sapphire, cobalt, indigo, lapis, aquamarine, cerulean, and some without names, twisted and stabbed at the sky. A black fissure ripped open, creating an inviting gateway to hell. The whispers became piercing screams. A pinpoint of cerulean pushed through the gash of black, expanding and intensifying.

Through her weakened vision, the Lady could see and feel the vehemence of the colors, flashing like a kaleidoscope. And she was not afraid of the demonic chorus; she had been to hell and back. The dot became a spinning sphere pushing through the crevice. It finally exploded, and the sound was deafening.

Floating above the Lady of Badb was an ethereal being assembled entirely of blue light, except for the floating gray robes drifting around her in a silken haze. The Lady's senses ignited, and her *vision* was clearer than when she was alive.

When the Goddess Nicnevin spoke, her otherworldly form solidified, but the slightest movement caused her face to morph entirely. She manifested three unique formations as if indecisive about which to choose. A maiden who exuded hope and opportunity with the aroma of spring. The face of a strong sexual woman, seducing all into her presence with the heat of summer—mother. Or a wise, haggard crone cut through with deep lines and winter's cold, heavy with shadows. All offered answers for a price.

She was fierce and unpredictable in every form.

Her power was immortal.

Daughter of torment. The shuddering and shattering of your soul, so agonizing and sharp, was a symphony to my Sluagh, and they want you.

They whisper that you should be one of them. My dark demons, my angels, my Sluagh na marbh. They hunger for you, and they don't ask for such lightly.

DELEVAN HOUSE

Like you, I have many names—Witch, Faerie Queen, Hecate, Gyre Carlin, Queen of Elphame, Neamhain, Mother, and Crone. I am Nicnevin.

And I have come, daughter, to your call of suffering. My Sluagh are never wrong with the music of anguish.

Her lips did not move when she spoke, yet the words flowed like water into The Lady of Badb. Her faces continued to flicker, but she had an absolute serenity. This specter thoughtfully regarded the corpse below, a smoky blue vision face-to-face with the ashen body streaked with the crusted brown blood of the last soldier to take her.

You're not finished with this realm, pale one. I can give life again. I can grant you what you need.

"I need them to pay," the parched corpse rasped.

Then you shall make them pay for as long as your hunger desires. You may take your revenge for eternity.

When the specter descended into The Lady of Badb, her infinite power was absorbed by the decomposing body lurching violently in the dirt. The Goddess Nicnevin whispered within the corpse's shell, infusing it with her essence.

Stringy muscles instantly became strong around bones. Shriveled veins and arteries filled, red once again with *life*. Vital human organs formed fully, then shifted into place. As the Lady regained her captivating beauty, her creamy skin glowed with vibrant health. Her green eyes were clear, and their dynamic energy vibrated through the air, filling it with static. Several birds fell from the sky, decorating the heather with their feathers, and the earth pulled them in for fuel.

When Nicnevin was satisfied with the transformation, the shape of her being reformed, and a toothless old woman grinned at the radiant resurrected beauty. The Lady of Badb sat on the ground, gently stroking the skin of her arms with her fingertips, marveling at the dark gift.

Nicnevin spoke with authority.

Your thirst for blood transcends human notions of petty revenge. You will feed on them all for as long as your desire persists. I, Nicnevin, your Queen and immortal Mother, gift fresh life to you from my Royal Court of the Unseelie. We shall meet when angels battle, and you may come to court. The Na Fir Chlis is a gateway; look to that which lies between, and you will have your siblings. You are now my daughter, the huntress, a Baobhan Sith, and one of my Unseelie children.

Black tendrils curled, melding together in the air behind Nicnevin. A second tear ripped through the universe, and through it, a gaggle of geese poured forth, vanishing into the form of the Goddess. She smiled at the blood-curdling sound of pulsating coils streaming through the opening, surrounded by waves of dancing green and blue lights. A doorway emerged.

The newly re-formed Lady of Badb instinctively reached for her ears.

Listen, daughter, said Nicnevin. *These are the voices of our court. Their welcoming chorus is for a new sister. They frolic in celebration of you.*

The Lady cautiously removed her hands from her ears. Her senses were alive, and the screeching transformed into a symphony—for her. Accepted. Tears welled in her eyes, remembering her human life and how she had been discarded. The voices fuelled her desire to inflict revenge and take back from the evils of her past. She wasn't human. She was something beyond any meager mortal comprehension.

DELEVAN HOUSE

Daughter. You are reborn. Reimagined as a Blood Goddess. You are a creature of the fae. A child of the Unseelie, and in every way, superior to the abomination that is mankind.

Nicnevin smiled a macabre crescent moon, an all-consuming black maw that could swallow the world if she desired. The Lady felt love for her new mother. Her immortal family sang to her from the crack between the worlds.

Her salvation would be born of demons and chaos.

One of the tendrils twisted into a tangle of knots. There was a suffocating swirl of smoky blackness, and from it fluttered a great black bird. It swooped through the air, and shards of blue and green glittered like stardust. The magnificent bird landed in the pit where her coffin lay open. It plucked up the noose buried with her body so long ago. When she saw the rope used to choke her pathetic, sad life from her body, The Lady rubbed at her neck. Her eyes filled with tears, burning with the pain of the moment she stepped off the wooden stool in her tiny shack of a home. She heard the tearing of skin as she swung, straining hard against the rope's death grip. Her ultimate sin saw her ostracized, even in death, and tossed into the ground—unceremoniously interred far away from the consecrated ground and the people of her village.

The bird retrieved the noose and swooped towards the Lady of Badb, landing squarely on her shoulder with its thick scaly black toes curled and black nails pressing against her white skin. The rope circled her neck, and she began to panic.

Be at peace, Daughter. This is a gift.

Coarse hemp slithered and scratched around her neck, then draped down to her breasts. Nicneven pressed her long bony fingers over the ends of the rope. Her nails were like the talons of the crow silently perched on the Lady's shoulder. The Fae Queen touched The Lady's chest over her heart.

The heart said nothing.

Not a shudder.

Not a whisper.

But it was there in a new form.

The rope tightened, transforming itself into a solid chain of silver. Her lips vibrated as The Fae Queen recited incantations in a language unknown to The Lady. Nicnevin's eyes turned inwards, becoming opal moons shining in the dark. She threw her head back as a wave of the aurora's light shot through her skull, and her skin pulsed with colors, intensifying when they reached her icy fingers. Another blast of immortal energy crashed from Nicnevin's hands into the Lady of Badb.

An eerie green glow emanated from her fair skin.

This is your key to our court and to me. Never part with it. I shall always be with you, daughter.

The noose of the rope Nicnevin held changed into a spectacular necklace of pure silver. It gleamed in the starlight. Shaped like a teardrop, intricately braided strands encased a spectacular green stone. The power it contained was strong, and the jewel burned hot against The Lady's skin.

This necklace holds your freedom and is a direct line to the court. It must never find its way into the possession of another.

The spectacle of Unseelie dancers shifting restlessly in the intense waves of blue that framed a glorious borealis dissolved into nothing as the Goddess silently faded back into the heavens.

DELEVAN HOUSE

The Lady rested on the soft peatland with her crow and her gifts, caressing the priceless gem. It is the eye of a living galaxy, swirling with magicks and captured lightning.

A piece of our realm.

The Lady bows her head as a single tear of gratitude for her new life slides down her cheek.

The bird, still perched upon the Lady, cawed in her ear, and she heard its name, *Fraoch*.

He was hers, and she was his.

This is where her true *life* began.

She was no longer the long-forgotten and disgraced sinner or a dead beauty unable to refuse the vile sins of men.

The Lady was now the feared and flesh and blood-thirsty *Baobhan Sith*. The huntress and seductress of men.

She roamed the highlands with Fraoch, her Unseelie corvid. Campfire stories told of a pair of crows—one black, the other hooded. Harbingers of death. Whispers of an otherworldly beauty of the night, swathed in green silk, fluttering behind her flawless body like wings. With unholy intentions in her eyes. Sex was an appetizer, and sanguine fluid was her main course.

She indulged her desires without fear or regret and knew satisfaction, at least for spells, until she needed to hunt and feed again.

Bodies discarded by the fiend of the highlands were found drained of blood with their eyes pecked out by her ghastly familiar. Fraoch's taste for the chewy orbs matched The Lady's for sex and blood.

They roamed together, seducing, killing and feeding without mercy for almost one hundred years. When she attacked the Laird Malcolm Delevan while he was hunting stag, something in his aristocratic blood prevented her from sucking him dry. She wanted to savor this handsome man and hold him under her spell—her handsome beast. She glamoured the mortal, so he would forget the attack. And unleashed another method of seduction. Stalking him, leading him to her...

Without memory of her original name, The Lady gave herself one—Lenore. She plucked it from the air. *What's in a name really*? Her kind went by many, even her Queen—Nicenevin, Nicneven, Neamhain, The Dark Queen, Daughter of Frenzy, Queen of the Unseelie, Sluagh Queen, Bone Mother, Gyre Carlin, Mother of the Wild Hunt, Faerie Queen. She decided such things didn't matter, only that she appeared more human to him. She wanted him to cry out *Lenore* when she made him scream.

Laird Malcolm Delevan was bewitched by The Green Lady from the minute he saw her brushing her luxurious hair by a burn, naked except for sturdy leather hunter's boots. He would've done anything to have her for himself. She laughed when he kneeled, so captivated by her that he promised her his undying love and devotion. The connection between the pair was immediate; neither could make sense of it, but she accepted his offer to make her his bride.

Her power over him rivaled the human definition of love. Dusted with a glimmer from her past life—hope.

DELEVAN HOUSE

They hand-fasted at Anand Castle on the edge of the cliffs as waves crashed against the ragged rocks below. Elements of nature collided in that hour, and rain poured down. Their union caused a storm that lasted for days.

Laird Delevan brought his bride to his home, Delevan House. The magnificent mansion overlooked the rural village of Badb. He owned the land there and tended to the residents with thoughtful consideration, ensuring their dues to him were paid. The residents respected their Laird, but the appearance of a mysterious new wife caused unease and much gossip.

A quiet conflict simmered unchecked.

Wolf Moon

2017

Dropping out of school was something Elspeth's family would not support; she had to get away from their obligations and pressures until she decided what to tell them. In reality, the cozy bothy on the Isle of Macha looked like one of those sad little remains of houses abandoned during the clearances of the Highlands and Islands in library books.

The foundation of the tiny abode was warped. The single-story gray stone shack slumped into the land, and the roof hung off to one side, barely visible. It was covered in greenery, intent on consuming it. The door was its strongest feature, made from heavy oak that matched the tiny re-framed windows.

Elspeth had fallen asleep slumped on the small, chunky sofa in front of the rustic brick fireplace, with nothing but the sound of the logs crackling and the intermittent ghostly howls of wind running through the small shack.

A loud thump jerked her rudely awake, and she threw a scratchy woolen blanket to the stone floor, startled and confused. *Was the noise a dream or the wind?* Elspeth stood up and stretched her arms above her head, lengthening her back, folded over, and touched her toes and back up again. *It must've been the wind.*

DELEVAN HOUSE

There was no one close by; she was in sweet isolation, which was exactly what she needed.

She was startled by furious scratching at the door. Elspeth shivered. Grabbing her shawl from the floor and throwing it around her shoulders, she walked to the small window near the door. The scratching stopped. Shifting the curtain to one side, Elspeth peered through the reflections of the bothy out into the dark. She only saw black, peering skyward. The clouds rolled and shifted, and light poured down, illuminating the land. The clouds continued to slide, and starlight pricked the sky. She had never seen so many. Elspeth smiled. *Who knew the night sky could be so bright.* She suddenly wanted to feel the magick of that silvery light on her skin and didn't care that it was cold out. She dropped the shawl, wearing only her ex-girlfriend's favorite slinky vest. Elspeth unlatched the door, and stepped barefoot onto the paving stones. They were freezing, and her feet grew numb, but she craved raw freedom and the night's glow on her body.

Then she heard the sound. An indisputable bone-chilling snarl of a vicious predator. She froze. A 7-foot snarling beast stood to her right on its hind legs. A wolf standing like a man. Its ears stood straight up, tilting back and forth, its snout wrinkled, baring teeth, drool dripping from its black lips, ready to pounce.

Freeze, fight, or flight. There was no way she could fight, and Elspeth was too fierce a woman to freeze and be torn apart by the beast. With only a split-second to choose, she ran.

Her feet thrashed through the barren land of a wretched place where the earth was coarse and uneven. A cluster of moss among the hard mounds, thick enough to weaken the ankles, tugged at her skin. Her soles were black and bloody, and the dirt absorbed the blood like an offering.

It knew her taste as a lover would. Elspeth battered through the harsh growth with stinging nettles nipping and nicking her calves. Angry welts spattered her fair skin, sharp thorns scratched like teeth. Her long dark hair was a messy spray like a hand-spun shawl of coal behind her. The young woman's ragged breathing signaled her panic. *It's gaining on me.* Nothing recognizable to hear or see, but she sensed it was close, and if it caught her, the wild beast would rip her apart.

The clouds swallow the pregnant moon, and light is extinguished, snuffed like a candle flame. Elspeth stumbled over a dip, lost her footing, and cried as pain radiated through her leg. A snap, and then she fell hard, catching her cheekbone on a black rock. Warm blood blossomed, pouring down her face as it painted the rocks red. Struggling to remain conscious, an unearthly howl shattered her suffering. Elspeth scanned the motionless perimeter as a shimmer of silver bled through the edges of the smothering sky.

A large cat slunk from between a thicket of ivy to the right, strutting towards her—slow and sure. It stopped. The creature had a wild look, larger than any domestic cat. Large ears, sharp triangles of skin, with wild silvery tufts caught the light. Wet nostrils flared, floating above her face before its rough, sandpaper tongue lapped at her wounded cheek. Apart from those shimmering tufts, the beast was blacker than night, with a strong silhouette, heavy paws, and a curiously short tail. It regarded her through striking chartreuse eyes with unflinching curiosity, laying a paw possessively over her hand.

Another howl from behind.

DELEVAN HOUSE

Elspeth gasped, and the beast nudged her chin with a head as big as her own, looking to the source. Sharp claws extended on her forearm, pressing for her attention.

Should I follow it?

There was no time to consider her options. She pulled herself up and followed the beast towards a thick cascade of ivy. The animal weaved between the curtain of green stars. Nothing could compare to the unseen terror that pursued her in the dark and moved closer. She submitted to the lesser evil and continued without glancing back.

Elspeth squeezed her body between curtains of greenery against what felt like a solid wall. It scratched at her skin, clammy and cold. Her senses had been firing beats of panic since the beast chased her from the bothy. *Bothy.* A nice word for the shack she was presented with upon arrival. The images online romanticized the accommodation in its description. Elspeth was sucked in by poetic words and pictures of scenic views on the listing. The price was too good, as things often are, to meet the claims. But she was desperate in her need for freedom.

Elspeth followed the giant cat towards an archway, revealing the red door of a heavy-set stone cottage. A soft glow emanated from two storm lights lit at either side of the entrance. The cat strutted through the door. Its short tail swishing with intention. Elspeth hesitated; the terror was still coursing through her, and her skin was damp with perspiration. She followed, gingerly stepping up the two steps and through the doorway.

"H-h-hello?" Her voice didn't sound like it belonged to her.

NATASHA SINCLAIR AND RUTHANN JAGGE

The hallway was dark, but the walls were adorned with rich wood paneling. She noticed a stairwell to the right and a sitting room to the left. Her bloody bare feet marked the hardwood floor with each step.

Peridot moons watched from another open door. The cat purred, and she followed the sound.

The teapot on the stove whistled. Elspeth tumbled from the sofa, smashing her arm on the coffee table.

"Fffffucker," she hissed, sucking in her breath and rubbing her bone.

"You ok?" A stranger's voice called from another room. *Where in hell am I?* Elspeth scratched her head. Her heart raced as her bruised body recalled the terror and exhaustion that pushed her into a restless sleep before her mind could put the pieces together.

A young woman glided into the room. Floor-length green lace billowed over the simple black linen dress she wore. Her face was smooth and unblemished, except for a few freckles. Her unusual green eyes were lined with kohl, making her less other-worldly than she appeared. Her eyes shone like gems in her pale face.

"How's the head?" she asked, setting down a tray of tea and bannocks. The aroma of the freshly baked treat calmed Elspeth's nerves a bit.

I'm sorry, but who are you? Where am I?"

DELEVAN HOUSE

"Take your time. Have sweet tea and a bite. You'll find your bearings soon enough. I promise."

A huge white bird swooped in, landing on the woman's shoulder. Elspeth jumped back, startled.

"Wooow there." The lady raised her hand in peace. "It's ok. This is Mauve. She's my personal angel. Wouldn't hurt a fly. Here." The young woman gestured for Elspeth to lean forward, but she shook her head.

"Sorry. I'm not really a bird person."

"Oh. Mauve isn't a typical bird." There was an air of distinct offense in her tone. "She's special. Open your palm in front of her. Go on." Her voice was encouraging, but her expression was suddenly cold.

Green eyes... there's something about green eyes.

Elspeth did as she was asked, nervously leaning closer to the huge white bird on the strange lady's shoulder.

Mauve tilted her head from side to side as her vivid turquoise orbs assessed Elspeth before lowering her white head down onto Elspeth's hand.

After rubbing its soft snowy plumage repeatedly, the bird rested her chin on Elspeth's palm. A chittering sound vibrated from a sizable pink beak—over three inches in length. Elspeth smiled and glanced at the woman who was watching intently. Elspeth's fears and worries disappeared as she gently stroked the bird with her finger.

"Does this mean she likes me?"

"She does."

"I have never seen anything like her. She's amazing. What is she, a parrot?"

"No. Mauve is a crow."

"Wow. I thought those were always black."

"Usually, they are. But not everything here is *usual*...."

Elspeth nodded.

Mauve, the white crow, settled again on her owner's shoulder. She reached for her teacup, and Elspeth did likewise. The steaming drink gave her strength.

"Well, now that you and Mauve have been introduced, I'm Caoimhe."

"Oh. I'm being rude, and you've been so kind. What a beautiful name. I'm Elspeth, but folks call me Eli."

"Pleasure to meet you, Eli."

The Isle of Macha was secluded. Caoimhe was the only permanent resident on the island, and apart from a private party that leased the run of the island monthly, she was entirely alone when she stayed here. Her garden produced enough for most meals, and there was easy access to rabbits when she craved a stew. Apart from her and the monthly visitors, there were no other predators, so their population flourished along with the wild sheep and goats. Though Caoimhe had no taste for meat from the cloven-hoofed.

And now, she had Elspeth. The young woman was running away from an unsatisfying life. Something in this house, on this island, with this stranger and her white crow, compelled her to stay.

Elspeth became a permanent fixture on the Isle of Macha.

Bringing Down the Flowers

1667

There was a room deep in the core of Delevan House reserved for a particular spell. The procedure did not necessarily require the energy of magicks. Some cunning folks dealt in concoctions of herbs that promised to bring back the regular blood course in earlier stages. Such methods weren't guaranteed, and the results were difficult to hide in intimate living situations. This was a need that only desperate women requested.

Some would try to take care of an unwanted in bloom in other ways, but those methods tore away the woman's life. A steep payment for an alleged sin. Lady Lenore Delevan's skills were exceptional, and she never turned a woman away.

Lenore Delevan gave each woman what she asked for without question. They didn't care what happened afterward. Her payment was their waste, a precious commodity to Lady Lenore. None of them ever asked what became of the discarded products from their wombs. The less known, the better, and the easier to pretend that the blooming of new life never happened in the first place.

Camille Gordon was the last woman to seek this service from Lady Delevan before The Lady's confinement. Camille's husband, Lawrence, had his sights on the lands of Badb and the neighboring village of Anand. He had a rivalry with Laird

Malcolm Delevan and tried to tarnish him whenever possible, though his attempts always failed. For the most part, the villagers honored their Laird. He was fair, and since he and his mysterious Lady took up permanent residence on Badb, leaving behind Castle Anand to his sister's family, Badb flourished in many ways.

Camille made her way across the Badb territory during the night, crossing rough land where the serpent met the crow. This was a lonesome pilgrimage that most women would not choose to make unaided. Lenore Delevan never willingly mixed with the locals—they avoided her when she ventured into the center for provisions.

Camille Gordon could not be seen consorting with the wife of her husband's rival, or he would beat her black and blue and have her shamed for treachery. But she was desperate.

The wind howled through the bare branches, battering the flatlands. *This is the only way.* Her feet crunched on the wilted grass. Frost would be here by morning. An eerie orange glow covered the horizon, reflecting from the Sutherland furnaces.

She married Lawrence Gordon when she was fifteen. He wanted her older sister, but she was already spoken for. Lawrence never showed his wife affection, she was merely a token of his manhood, and marriage was necessary for his ambitions. Filling her belly with viable seed was his duty. No pleasure, desire or love existed between the two, only a document proclaiming ownership and obligation. As a Minister and Witch-Pricker of the community working between Badb, Anand Village and the Isle of Macha, he was often absent, busy with his duties in gathering key prosecution evidence, bearing witness, overseeing penalties, and executions. This work suited the twisted heart of a bitter man.

The Malleus Maleficarum was his mistress. A damned book. Since he obtained a copy, the man was obsessed. He worshiped the pages like he did his bible, reading slowly. He was careful to absorb each lesson. These words fuelled men with fear and hate, and they became hell-bent on control. It was precisely what her husband's soulless heart required. The book rarely left his hands. He even slept with his fingers fondling the leather jacket with more tenderness than he had ever shown Camille. The messages within outweighed the value of any wife to him.

He was never attractive, and his face hardened with each conviction; Lawrence Gordon was a picture of hate. He did not confide in women, let alone one he had no respect for and never loved, but Camille she knew more than she was comfortable with. She tried to find compassion for his position and a reason to care for him but failed.

He was a hateful man.

When he penetrated her in the dark, she'd lie stiff and in silence, holding back her disgust and disdain for the spiteful servant of God.

A case in Anand involved the trial of a family accused of numerous accounts of witchcraft. Lawrence Gordon had been working in villages and towns around the country for weeks. Although relatively close to the village of Anand, his work was intense, and the distance was too great to be home until he was finished.

While he was away, his young wife found herself in bloom. Blossoming with seed that she knew, if carried to fruition, would never pass as her husbands. Her love for another grew in her belly. She had no choice but to extinguish it, or her life would be forfeit. She made the lonely walk from her home during the night as her two young sons slept. Camille moved silently through the thick heathers, following the narrow path between the serpent and the crow, to Delevan House.

The heady fragrance of flowers was a marriage of Star Jasmine, Nicotiana and Moonflower. Their perfumes permeated the cold air, filling her nostrils. It didn't matter the season. The grounds here bore abundant supplies of flora and herbs unlike anywhere else. The scent washed away the stench of sulfur coming from distant iron furnaces. The rich botanicals guided her across the narrow duckboard path between the tails of Delevan Loch and Loch Badb. This ancient walkway only led to one place.

The waters rippled continuously from the wind skimming the mirrored surfaces in a love affair of air and water joined in continuous capillary waves.

Camille thought of her own experience with love. *Is the real thing always forbidden?* She carried the product of her one and only beloved in her belly. A grave sin outside of her unhappy marriage of convenience.

When she crossed the bridge-like path, twinkles of light lit up around the perimeter of the house. From the night-blooming flowers shone the light of mini-moons and stars scattered among the thick foliage. Above the house, a flock watched the woman's every step.

Her path was set.

These eyes saw and carried everything back to that destiny.

DELEVAN HOUSE

Camille walked the stone path that cut through a meadow, swaying with wild weeds. She was comforted by the stones of the House. They hummed with anomalous vibrations, intensifying through her feet the closer she moved toward the Delevan mansion.

Approaching the outer walls, Camille stopped; she had never been this close to Delevan House before. It was forbidden. Even on those days, the villagers came to pay their dues to Laird Delevan—her husband forbade her to attend.

Great stone monoliths guarded the perimeter. People shared stories about the giants. As a child, Camille was told that this stone circle was built by fae folk. Many myths about these fierce beings made young children and adults alike fearful of sleep.

Some say that the first settlers made a pact with the fae, and these monoliths rose from the dirt. Some say that changelings used to be left in the center before the house stood dominant in its place. Others say each family took a turn making a sacrifice in exchange for bountiful harvests for the village. Perhaps these fae folk were responsible for the rich ore veins threading beneath Badb. One detail materialized in every story—a call for blood.

Camille wandered through the gardens, taking in the oddly inviting place. Why such beauty was feared suddenly became absurd to Camille. Within the threshold of the standing stones, arches rose over her head as they worshipped the moon. *I wonder if people are merely jealous of the Laird and Lady? Of this House and their happiness.*

The grounds comprised mini gardens abundant with herbs, vegetables and exotic flowers. To the left of the house, she entered one dominated by Lavender. The scent was intoxicating, and her head spun in the purple haze. A sharp clack, then fluttering, broke her botanical delirium. She looked up. Small shiny marbles, darker than the night, caught the light of the moon and stared back at her. There were many crows roosting among the arches of the roofs and over windows.

"Come in, Camille Gordon, the door is open to you," called the Lady of the House.

The voice was unexpected, and Camille jumped. Even her voice was unique. Her accent seemed held lost, with no distinctive tilts and rolls of the native dialects. She wasn't foreign, but she wasn't of them either. *Who is she, really?* Camille shivered, pulling her well-worn red and green tartan shawl tighter around her shoulders and stomach, remembering why she was here. *It's the only way.* She ran her palm over her belly, then climbed three stone steps. Camille pushed open the heavy door and stepped into the dim light of Delevan House.

The woman before her stood tall, exuding elegance. She was a dream. The air around her was as perfumed as her impressive gardens. Her beauty was intimidating and rare; she was no commoner. The Lady was refined, a chiseled goddess shaped from the finest marble. Her chartreuse eyes matched her perfectly fitted floor-length gown. It was a simple garment, but on this woman, it was exquisite.

Camille stood just inside the threshold, between one life and another, between hers and the unborn. The emerald gaze of the Lady regarded her calmly. Camille began fidgeting with her woolen shawl and chewed the skin on her lower lip.

"M-m-my apologies for the late hour."

"None needed, Dear. I knew you'd come."

DELEVAN HOUSE

Camille considered how odd it was to find someone so put together at this hour. The Lady gestured to the open door behind Camille, and she gingerly closed it without taking her eyes off her hostess.

From the ample garden room with wood-paneled walls intricately carved with flowers that seemed to be growing out of and within the wood, Camille cautiously followed her silent hostess through the house. Lady Delevan's elegant walk made no sound. Only her long emerald gown swished on the parquet flooring.

Does she even breathe? Camille understood that she didn't have to think or worry anymore in this house. She had already made the decision to surrender. When crossing that bridge between the waters surrounding this place, she had willingly placed the fate of her unborn into the hands of the Lady.

Still intoxicated by the scents, her head felt lighter than ever. Hallways flowed from other hallways in no pattern at all. Warm light cascaded waterfalls from rushlights that were unlike any other—instead of being fashioned from the usual iron, these fixtures were carved from the stone of the house's bones. This was typical anywhere, but here in Badb, where the ore is plentiful, its processing and use by the local blacksmiths was a pride rooted in every family. Iron was expected. Camille noted there was none here.

She was led down a steep spiraling stairwell. The botanicals lingering in her nose were diluted by a musty dampness. *Could we be beneath one of the lochs? How could any house here have subterranean rooms?* Questions rolled through Camille's mind, replacing her urgency to visit the House.

Camille ran her fingers along the walls. She was compelled to touch and feel their texture. Finally, they entered a room shaped like a black moon hollowed out from the earth. The walls were heavy with shelving and filled with jars and bottles of herbs and oddities.

I'm in the company of a witch! A criminal! She considered what her husband would do. This discovery would bring him the power he craved and destroy his rival, Malcolm Delevan. He would execute his wife, this remarkable Lady, and Camille would suffer too.

"Yes, your husband would not be pleased. But he'd best not test my patience. I'm much more than such men know of the word *witch*."

Camille was shocked *she heard my thoughts!* But Lady Delevan's eyes sparkled. She was awash with calm.

"A cunning woman would gain your confidence with a beverage and pleasantries, but we know why you are here. Time is too precious to waste, is it not?"

"Yes. There is no time. Is it true that it will all be over on this night? There will be no lingering effects?"

Lenore Delevan held a candelabra in her right hand. Her illumination was the only light in the room. Her face was the only thing Camille could see; this strange woman was the object of her salvation, *my dark Angel*. Her skin prickled with a fear she could not shake. She was inside the den of a predator.

"Do you trust me?" The Lady cawed, and her pupils were pinpoints to oblivion.

"I fear you." Camille swallowed.

Lenore glided back effortlessly beside her. Even the flame in her hand didn't flicker.

DELEVAN HOUSE

"Do you trust that I can remove your burden? This burden?" Lenore placed her left palm over the rise of Camille's belly.

"I do. You are the only thing I can trust right now."

"Then it shall be taken care of, dear one. It shall be concluded before you depart my threshold." The calming chill of her slender hand on her body created a peculiar longing deep within Camille. When she removed it and glided towards the wood-topped counter at the head of the room, candles, on all sides, sparked to life.

Flames licked the air, casting dancing shadows around them. Lenore Delevan took a pestle and mortar from the counter and selected ingredients from the array of jars and vials. Grinding them together, she added warm liquid. Heat rose from the concoction. It was not ordinary steam. It shimmered, violet in color, as it circled the room.

"Please have a seat on the table." Lenore's tone was commanding. Camille stepped up onto a small stool resting beneath the round table. Her dress slid across the smooth wood as she shuffled her bottom over the edge. It was beautifully decorated with carvings, and Camille was impressed by the ornate table in this secret room hidden deep in the bowels of the House.

The carvings formed an ornate band of symbols, detailed in knotwork around the table's circumference, giving it a distinctly altar-like quality.

Have I walked into a trap? Will this witch sacrifice me to her Devil? Panic fluttered through Camille's chest. She lifted her hand to her face and caught a strong mint-like aroma. The sweetness knocked back her doubt as it calmed her mind.

"No, Camille. I have no Devil. Your problem shall be resolved tonight. Please lie back."

Like an obedient dog, she slid her body back and lay on the table. Her host selected a rounded clay cup from the lower shelf before her and strained the elixir into it while whispering quietly.

Lady Delevan removed her patient's mud-caked boots and came around to her head. She perched the cup on the table by Camille's shoulder. Spreading her cold palms over the woman's temples, her fingers slithered down her cheeks, curling beneath Camille's jaw. Lady Delevan gazed into the young woman. When she saw the eyes of the unborn looking back through behind its sealed near-translucent lids, she recognized the soul of one conceived in betrayal and forbidden love, her favorite kind.

Camille was mesmerized by the hypnotic green waves in Lenore's eyes. She could hear the ocean as if she was standing with her bare feet sinking into grainy sand with water lapping at her ankles. This rhythmic motion slowed the rapid beating of her heart. Her breathing calmed. Lenore lifted Camille's head and raised the cup to her lips. Camille was parched by the salty sea manifested in the Lady's eyes.

"Drink," she insisted. Camille obeyed. She swallowed deeply from the small cup. The liquid was cool and coated her mouth and throat like honey, though it was intensely mentholated and floral, like drinking a liquid bouquet. The elixir stung the thin skin of her lips, and her tongue numbed. The Lady's lips moved again in a silent spell, and Camille's ears were filled with the cackle of crows.

DELEVAN HOUSE

Cold raced through her veins, and she gasped, arching her neck and clawing the table. Lady Lenore gently placed Camille's head back down on the table. Her tension eased.

Lenore moved around the table, stroking the etched edges with her fingers until she was back at the foot of her prey. Her hungry hands traced up Camille's legs pushing thick woolen skirts around her waist. She eyed the gateway of life, the woman's swollen sex, then burrowed her face between her pale thighs. Lenore pierced Camille with her tongue, prodding and lapping her insides as her serpent's tongue forked, rooting for the opening of her softening cervix.

Camille trembled. Her spine arched, Lady Lenore clutched at the swollen belly and began kneading through the waves of Camille's pain. Camille strained as her spine flexed, her body spasming against the woman's cold grasp. She felt herself opening. Hot blood flowed like a tide from Camille's body into the demanding mouth of Lady Delevan, the Baobhan Sìth.

Lenore pulled her face away from Camille's body, growing taller. Her eyes were the blood-red of a harvest moon, and her lips shone with her juices.

"She's coming. It'll be over soon," the sorceress rasped.

Birth was imminent. A deathly stillness blanketed the room.

Camille Gordon was delirious. She imagined herself asleep, alone in her four-poster bed in the comfort of her home. A final intense contraction tore through her abdomen and pelvis. She was overcome with nausea, and her body contracted violently, expelling the fetus into the open palms of Lenore Delevan. Camilla sobbed.

"Shush, Dear. Close your eyes and listen to the birds."

Sniffling, Camille rubbed the heels of her palms hard into her eyes and squeezed shut as tight as she could. She heard the birds.

Behind closed lids, she leaned into the sound as it intensified. Her mind soared, and she floated around the House and village with their birds-eye view.

Lenore Delevan eyed the infant in her hands, bound to its mother by the twisted umbilical rope. Its fate was sealed when Camille bedded a man outside wedlock and when she trudged through the dark beneath the obsidian observances and curious stars to Delevan House.

Lenore covered the baby's mouth and nose with her lips wide and sucked its single breath of innocence into her body. The pure breath was euphoria. Lenore plummeted from a great height, at high speed with no ground in sight, as that pure first and last breath flooded her body. The Lady reveled in the pleasure until it subsided.

Lenore Delevan plucked her ceremonial sgian-dubh from her dress pocket and sliced through the fibrous chord against the table. Camille was still. Lenore dropped the knife as fresh blood sprayed, and her insatiable thirst bathed her green eyes with red. She sucked on the severed ends. The deathly cold inside her warmed.

Lenore turned from Camille and nestled the tiny body inside a carved wooden box. She caressed it with her fingers. *"Mauve," she whispers.* A thin plume of misty-white smoke rose up, penetrating the stones of Delevan House. The vapor rose and danced through the highest rooms, curling seductively like a serpent until it exited the spired roof into the chill of the night. The waiting murder of crows celebrated with cacks, taps

DELEVAN HOUSE

and caws, forming a magnificent display. They fluttered in a stygian cloud, enveloping Delevan House in their music that echoed over the chilly planes of land and lochs. The sound echoed through every house and building in Badb and beyond. The sound of an unborn delivered up as one of them—another soul fused to Lady Delevan.

Camille was still motionless, apart from ragged breathing that caused her abdomen to quiver. Lenore hooked her arms under Camille's thighs and pulled her forward. She vigorously massaged Camille's lower abdomen with her forearm and hand as if kneading dough. She squeezed until the woman's body expelled the thick meat of glistening placenta.

The Lady must feed.

Lenore catches a reflection of her Dark Queen, Nicnevin, in the shimmering gore. Cobalt frames her face and the terrifying screeches of her Sluagh na marbh, scrape at the edges of Lenore's mind. Her hunger intensifies.

Lenore cracks her neck from side to side. The bones and muscles in her spine pop. The sound ricochets off the stones. The Lady devours the meat, tearing into the thickly veined flesh. Blood squirts into her dry throat. Death ravages her body when she is hungry until she feeds, filling her shell of her with blood. This blood is close to the ichor of the old ones. Magick in the meat melts the pain of her death away, imbuing her with *life* again. Lady Lenore Delevan is renewed. The dark Goddess who walks the earth.

NATASHA SINCLAIR AND RUTHANN JAGGE

Camille Gordon woke with a start, alone in her marital bed. Dawn stuttered through the window, sluggish and dull, like her awakening. *How....* Her mind and sight were clouded with a thick fog. Her fingers clutched at the soft bedding, remembering the feel of carvings in wood. *What did they say?*

She still wore the clothes from her forbidden errand. Mud caked her skirts and was crusted between the toes of her bare feet. Camille ran her hands over her belly. The bump was no longer. Her womb was empty and shrunken. *It was true. She took it away.* She was empty inside again.

A clack and rap-tap at the window startled her. A peculiar bird tapped at the thin pane. Its large beak was pink, and it had snow-white feathers. It looked and sounded like a corvid. *A white crow?* Camille had never known such a bird to exist. It frightened her. Its tapping grew more incessant, cracking the glass.

Beady turquoise eyes stared at the woman, head tilting with curiosity. She mimicked the bird's movement, captivated by the creature. Camille blinked, and the white crow was gone.

Her husband would be home soon.

A band of mellow light glimmered above the misty horizon. It was said that such displays of magick were a window between this world and Elphame—Faerie.

Lady Lenore Delevan felt the darkness changing to light deeply. Her position beneath the earth had no impact on the energy shifting between the gap in the sky.

DELEVAN HOUSE

She touched the miniature casket again, fingering the name she had carved into the wood using the sharp point of her nail. *Mauve.* She touched her lips softly, whispering, feeling the motion of the swirling script on her lips. *Mauve.* Lenore placed the casket in an opening in the wall, carefully pushing it back until she was elbow-deep in the cavity. She placed a heavy chunk of stone into the space, then another, concealing the opening completely. Interring the body in the private tomb of Delevan House. With her razor-sharp fingernail, she effortlessly scored sigils into the solid rock.

Lawrence Gordon rode in front of his companions from his village. His chestnut stallion, Murphy, showed no signs of weariness, unlike his master. He had been gone for more than three months. The trials were plenty and satisfying. He regarded himself to be a hand of God during these times of diabolism. The human race was at war with the Devil as he wound his way through the lives of good folk, using the filthy heathen hands of witches. Lawrence Gordon had dedicated his life to weeding them out.

His last case, in the neighboring village of Anand, was a trial on him as much as it was the guilty parties. He was called in for his skills as a pricker. His sharp instrument never failed to locate *the mark* that confirmed the allegiance of a witch to their Satanic master. Often disguised as a freckle or a mole—when rammed with his blessed instrument, the result would be a scream of innocence or the confirmation by the lack of reaction and blood from the pricked mark. He always found their marks, eventually. Secretly, Lawrence enjoyed the process. He knew that many simply ran out of tears from the pain of being processed so thoroughly, nontheless—guilty!

The last trial concerned the crimes of witchcraft by a mother and daughter. The daughter routinely shape-shifted into a pony and rode the mother around on her back as they committed their wicked crimes, which included cursing neighbors' crops and drying up the udders of valuable cattle. They became so intent on their heinous misdoings that the child could not entirely shift back, leaving her left hand and feet grotesquely misshapen—more hoof-like than any human should be. The mother rode her possessed daughter until she was lame. Neighbors reported seeing them out at night, at all hours, chanting at the moon and talking to unseen entities. The evidence concluded they were indeed engaging with Satan himself, although neither would admit to their crimes. On the eve of their execution, the daughter vanished as though swept away by the fiend, Lucifer, himself. It was the only *reasonable* explanation after the villagers and authorities searched for her and came up empty. The mother was tossed naked into a barrel, tarred and burned. Her execution was swift and just, but the issue of the missing girl did not sit right with Lawrence Gordon. The thought of a cloven heathen roaming the country made him physically ill.

Stopping at The Rowan for a few drams, Lawrence overheard gossip regarding his wife Camille, who was seen crossing the duckboards during the night. His bloodlust and hatred of all women were elevated. He would not have such disobedience in his village, let alone his home.

DELEVAN HOUSE

What ensued is documented in the vaults of the village library. More detailed accounts are held by the Gordons under lock and key.

Camille was accused and found guilty of fraternizing with a witch. Her trial and execution were swift, wrapped up in just forty-eight hours.

Death by strangulation, followed by burning. This was her husband's *mercy*.

The trial of the accused witch, Lady Lenore Delevan, was less straightforward, compounded by the abrupt and mysterious disappearance of Badb's beloved Laird. She was judged and processed using every punishment at their disposal. Lawrence Gordon also used some devised solely for her suffering. His only regret was that he was unable to also make an example of Laird Delevan for bringing this abomination into their lives.

When it was time to light her pyre, this witch of Badb would not burn. The flames flickered, then refused to ignite.

Her accusers had to resort to other means to entrap this demon—forever. Every generation, henceforth, would have a part to play. An accursed binding that would mark the village of Badb with eternal damnation.

Edge-Walker and the Gypsy

2020

Long shadows descend, and the gloom and glow of dusk tease the horizon. When the metallic smell of Badb is ripe in the damp mist, Pivona McQueeney notices a peculiar figure dancing on the shoreline in the wavering light as she strolls along the narrow paths. Always nosy and obnoxious, she pulls her wool fringes closer and eases herself toward potential excitement.

Her stomach rumbles. She needs to find a warm place to spend the night. The village thrives on gossip—valid or not. Rumors often take the place of meaningful conversation, feeding small minds and superstition. It's as if the residents are of a single mind at times, thriving on speculation. Pivona is only too happy to feed their appetites in exchange for hers—a few coins or a loaf of bread will often do.

There's an audience of corvids in the branches of the trees nearby, and their song guides her. The figure she's watching makes slow, deliberate circles in the air with a stick, tiptoes straining for an extra inch closer to the clouds as if writing a message in the sky. *It's a girl.*

Pivona can barely make out the curious girl's shape under her loose brown smock, but her long wispy hair flows behind her. It's the color of cornsilk and full of light, like the rising moon. She's singing—a sound between humming and croaking as she skips, and Pivona strains against the sounds of the sea, trying to recognize the tune.

The scene is unsettling, but Pivona inches closer. The girl's face is hard to define, her features are muted, and her figure has unnatural transparency. She's a ghost in the fog.

Despite the chill of the evening, the dancing girl's feet are bare, oblivious to the cold water lapping at her toes. The crows flutter in time with her movements, and others boldly swoop in close, grazing her hands with offerings. She accepts, tucking them into her pockets.

The willowy girl dips and whirls faster, moving away, dragging a stick behind her, etching patterns on the ground. When the girl lifts her arms in salute to the colors of the early sunset, Pivona notices an unusual green tinge rimming the sky. Shivering, she wraps her arms around herself, head bowed low in the shadows, but continues to stare. She's curious about this girl and especially interested in the gifts the corvids share with her. *They may be valuable.*

She watches intently as the birds return to the highest branches. They are motionless now, resting for the night.

It's harder to make out the shape of the dancing girl as dusk unfurls. Pivona isn't feeling up to chasing after her and questioning her tonight. Instead, she slides herself along the seawall, kicking at the rocks as she makes her way along the short path back to the village.

Lights flicker in the windows of the rustic, single-story cottages. She knows the back alley of The Rowan, a casual eatery and pub, is her best bet for a meal. Pivona positions herself off to one side of the entrance, making a nest of her layers of garments, the better to catch the attention of anyone coming or going.

Arlen Morven is dragging out a metal bin. When the lid clatters to the ground, Voni's startled cry causes the young man to lose his balance, landing in a heap of rubbish next to the giggling waif.

"Hello brat, you stink to high heaven, Voni, worse than this mess. When was your last scrub?" Arlen wipes smears of tomato sauce off his jeans, flicking scraps of lettuce at her. The two playfully toss handfuls of rubbish at each other until Pivona decides a discarded roll is still fresh enough to nibble on.

Arlen's good-looking, and she knows a few girls in the village who'd like to claim him. Still, he's made it clear that he's leaving Badb as soon as possible to pursue a career as a pharmacist or doctor. She wouldn't mind a few lessons from him. She likes how his red hair curls around his neck and imagines swirling it between her fingers as he kisses her. Pivona snuggles in close, but Arlen gently pushes her away.

"Last week, I dipped into the sea on a warmer day, I was naked to the world, but you missed it." She winks, but Arlen ignores her. "You won't believe what I saw over by the seawall just now." Pivona wiggles her eyebrows, pointing in the direction of the water. "Want me to tell you?" Arlen stands, reaching a hand down to the girl. He can't help but feel sorry for her. From what he knows of her situation, she has no one and nothing to rely on.

"You and your stories, Voni. Why don't you try learning how to stitch or bake? Some kind of skill that would buy you

DELEVAN HOUSE

a decent meal and some clothes? Don't you want to be respectable?"

"I'd enjoy a pretty dress. Would you take me out on a picnic then, Arlen, if I dressed like a *respectable* girl?" Pivona teases, but Arlen's face is serious. He's sure she doesn't know what could happen on a picnic with a man, but she knows how to flirt, which is dangerous.

"No, Voni. You need to get a lot smarter and fast. You don't want to spend nights in this or any other alley, hoping some drunk will toss coins for your favors. My Ma sews garments for the village and other special things, but she also takes in mending. I could bring you by the house tomorrow. Maybe she'll hire you to lend a hand with pressing."

"Nope. I'm a free spirit. I come from people no one can cage or control. I'll take my chances on my wits and devastatingly good looks to get me by." Pivona is pretty under the layers of grubby fabric, and her coal-black, tangled, matted hair still shines under the dull lights of the pub. Arlen frowns, shaking his head. Gathering the rubbish, he tosses the scraps back into the bin, dragging it to the curb, and then wipes his hands on the damp grass.

"Aren't you going to ask me what I saw?" Pivona is not ready to be alone just yet.

"What is it you think you saw, Voni? Your stories and lies usually don't amount to much, but you enjoy stirring the gossip-pot." Arlen's not interested in such things, although the pub is constantly buzzing with gossip. He's a loner who prefers to spend his free time hiking and making notes, sketching unusual plants and herbs he discovers in the wooded areas surrounding Babd. He fancies himself a type of scientist, distilling and brewing tinctures.

"Don't judge me, Arlen. Everybody knows your ma don't only take in mending. She also hands out little brown glass bottles to those looking for love or to get rid of it. She's well-known for her tansy tea with honey." Pivona explodes into laughter, puffing her belly and slapping Arlen on the arm. "You Morvens ain't so high and mighty." Arlen isn't laughing. His eyes narrow, and his body tenses, with fists clenched at his sides. For a split second, she fears he may strike her, and Pivona quickly changes her tune.

"So, there was this, I think, girl, down by the shoreline. She was making some kind of noisy racket and dancing under the birds. The funny thing is she was there, and then she was gone. I can't say what I saw for sure, but it looked like the crows swooped in to dance with her, and she took something from them." Arlen's eyebrows crinkle together in a frown, and his cheeks flush. Placing his hands firmly on Pivona's shoulders, he leans in close.

"Stay clear of this, Pivona. She's nothing you should meddle in or chatter about. The Threnody isn't a girl. She's not one of us. That creature is clairaudient, and I'm surprised you're still standing here to tell the story. Bad things happen whenever she shows up." Arlen's tone is harsh, and Pivona's eyes grow wide. The sighting might be the juicy tidbit she needs to be paid by those most interested in her information.

"Who is she, Arlen? Don't play with me?" Pivona tugs at the front of his denim shirt. "I need to know."

"Oh, she's something, all right, but I've said too much. I expect you'll learn for yourself soon enough. I have to go in

DELEVAN HOUSE

now. You take good care, Voni. I'll ask the cook to leave you a plate at the door." Arlen shrugs her off, closing the heavy door to The Rowan behind him. He doesn't want to hear another word. Frustrated, Pivona rattles the knob.

Pivona isn't concerned with Arlen's warning. The door squeals open again, and a thick forearm reaches out, offering a plate with a burger, chips and a cup of hot tea. The girl scrambles to accept the treat, mumbling her thanks, but the door slams firmly shut. It locks from the inside. She's no chance of getting in now. Sitting on the steps while sipping her tea, the girl realizes she'll need to find shelter against the coming weather. It's growing colder by the minute.

Maybe Arlen's right. I will stop by the Morvens' place tomorrow. Pivona McQueeney makes herself small for the night, pulling the layers she wears up and over her head for warmth and disguise as she huddles in the alley behind The Rowan. She never sleeps deep enough to dream and no longer believes in dreams.

The girl's a fixture in the village, everyone knows her story, and there's no real threat to her well-being, but folks are unpredictable this time of the year. No one is safe.

Dusting cobwebs from her eyes and mind, Pivona shakes herself awake at first light, and she's considerate enough not to do her business near the pub.

Babd is full of early risers, and steam from the forges trail through the narrow streets behind her like ghosts. She makes her way to a narrow plank dock where the water is frigid but shallow. The birds swoop overhead, their ebony eyes watchful as she splashes water on herself. *I'd best smell presentable if I'm asking for work.* The girl reaches into a leather pouch hanging at her waist. A scrap of mirror reflects back her sharp cheekbones and large brown eyes. Propping it up on a nearby rock, Pivona rakes her fingers through her wild mass of hair, weaving it into an intricate braid. A single tear slides down her caramel cheek. *I remember Mama doing this for me.* She doesn't feel sorry for herself as she chose to abandon her people and remain in Babd, but she hoped someone would return for her, ransom or not. They never did.

There's a light on in the window facing the street of the Morvens' house. Minerva Morven sits alone, skilfully stitching an intricate design on green silk. Voni gently knocks on the window, pressing her nose to the glass.

"Why are you bothering me so early, Miss McQueeney? I have important work to finish. Are you hungry or hurt? I don't have time for your tales this morning." Minerva's a widow, Arlen is her only son, and her husband died at sea many years ago. She's short and sturdy, with cropped brown hair, mousey features with soulful eyes. Her fingers are wrapped with lengths of green silk thread. Shining needles of different sizes pierce the bodice of her practical black dress. No one else in the village, or perhaps anywhere, has her exceptional skills, and she works long hours to support herself, often giving back to the community.

"Sorry to bother you. Arlen said you're needing a hand with the pressing. I can't sew, but I'm willing to try and learn. I don't need much. I want to make something of myself and maybe have a place to rest at night."

Minerva's eyes slide up and down the girl, taking in her worn cast-offs, but her hair is nicely braided, and her hands are clean. She knows the results of the damaging gossip Pivona spreads, but some company would be nice now that her boy is working and eager to be on his own.

"I won't allow games or nonsense, girl. You'll need to clean up your act if I take you on. I'm not sure you're one for work. I can't pay much, but there's a small room off the back that's almost empty." Minerva gestures to the side of the cottage with her head. "Get rid of some of those rags and junky trinkets, and come back tomorrow. I'll make up the bed and have things ready for you then." Pivona grins. She fingers the bits of broken jewelry and shiny scraps dangling around her neck on ribbons and thin chains, she thinks they're pretty, and she's worn some of the decorations and amulets for years. "I can't promise I'm a perfect teacher, but I won't do you wrong." Pivona claps her hand excitedly, nodding in agreement.

"Thank you, Minerva. I'm going to try hard."

"And Miss McQueeney? My son is off-limits. He's not part of our arrangement, so stay away from him. He works hard and has plans. He doesn't need a distraction teasing him."

"Arlen's been kind to me, but I ain't looking for a man." Pivona winks at the woman.

"Tomorrow, then." Minerva nods briskly, dismissing the girl. She has doubts but hopes Pivona will make an effort.

It had been a while since Pivona had the comfort of a bed, even though it was narrow and hard. A small chest of drawers with a scratched mirror, a glass jar of fresh-cut Peonies and a few clean towels made the closet-sized room luxurious in her mind. Minerva, true to her word, made space for her.

Pivona's day was spent sitting close to Minerva, watching as she expertly stitched layers of fine green silk. Her task was to snip through the tiny basting stitches on a delicate linen garment, taking care not to nick the thin fabric in the process.

"Slow your mind and focus on the work. Not everything needs to be desperate and fast in life." Minerva is patient. She wants to give the sketchy young teen a chance but expects her to do her part. "There's fish stew on the stove and a chunk of good bread you can have for dinner. I'm off to my sewing circle tonight and will be back late."

Once a month, Minerva meets with a trusted circle of women who carry the burdens of the surrounding villages and hamlets as healers and advisors. They've gathered together for many years at a stone cottage near the water, sharing concerns and potential solutions.

"Can I come along?" Pivona is eager to be included. She's betting such get-togethers are full of entertaining information too.

"No. This is *my* time with old friends. There's powdered soap under the sink. Give your undies a soaking, then hang them to dry in the night air. It's my secret for making fabric smell extra clean." Minerva didn't own a washing machine, preferring to do her laundry out back and then hang things on the line like most in the village.

Badb isn't quick to adapt or change, and some things many take for granted, aren't readily available there due to its remoteness. Pivona nods.

"Arlen is working a lot and doesn't come home much anymore. I suspect he's got or is looking for a girl." Pivona smirks, but Minerva's tone is sharp. "I told you he's off limits. You won't bother him if you want to stay on my good side. He's a good boy and will go to university in Edinburgh. He may

DELEVAN HOUSE

even become a doctor. He doesn't need an easy piece ruining everything." She taps a finger on the chemise Pivona is holding. "You've missed three stitches here. Pay attention and do it right." Pivona nods. She's already decided to visit Arlen in spite of Minerva's warning.

Being naked doesn't bother Pivona. Choosing a spot on the banks of the serpent (Delevan Loch), she kneels in the early evening breezes, wrapped only in a towel from her room. The girl carefully washes her small garments, but there's little left of the threadbare cotton. Having clean underclothes will be a treat. *I'll buy new things when I am paid, or maybe Minerva can teach me to make something pretty.* Having something to look forward to feels good, and she doesn't notice Arlen standing behind her.

"For the love of— put something on, girl!" Sliding his leather jacket off, he bends to wrap it around her narrow shoulders. "It was my dad's, so don't be thinking it's yours to keep. You can't be out here like this. Someone might see you or worse. I won't always be around to have your back." Pivona smiles up at him. "I came down to check a fishing line I set out earlier, and here you are with your arse in the breeze. I need to get back to work, but make sure to leave my jacket at the back door of The Rowan when you're through here."

"Can't we have a chat?" Pivona sniffs the cracked leather, breathing in the smell of him on the worn jacket, but she's embarrassed to be holding her shabby wet clothing.

"No time. I'll see you soon." With a nod, he's gone, leaving the teen with her imagination and his jacket. Dressing quickly, she panics for a minute, thinking that her necklaces are gone, then remembers that she's no longer wearing them. She feels more exposed without her charms than in her bare skin, but the weight of Arlen's jacket is soothing.

Squeezing her clothes one last time into the lapping water, Pivona catches sight of the strange girl again, standing on a tall black rock not far from her.

The loose brown smock she wears billows as she slowly spirals in circles. Her footing is as steady as a ballerina's. She's singing again, a peculiar sound without words. Her features are sharp and delicate. Pivona notices an arrangement of circles and lines drawn in the rough sand.

"Hello, I'm Voni. I've seen you here before. Do you live in the village?"

Carrying her damp clothing in one hand, she inches her way over the sharp pebbles toward the stranger.

The girl pauses, looking directly at Pivona, but a mob of crows descends from trees near the rock, their wings glittering in the evening light. There are dozens of them. One plummets, grazing Pivona's cheek with its sharp beak, while others move in, closing the gap between her and the girl. Pivona is taken aback, but the girl isn't afraid. She holds out her open palms, accepting small stones in every shade of green from them. Pivona is fascinated.

One at a time, the birds gently drop their treasure into the girl's waiting hand, and she wonders if the stones are gems and valuable.

"What's your name, and what kind of stones are they?" Pivona is close to her now, watching the girl's expressionless face for a smile or greeting, but her eyes are empty pools. "We can be friends if you like, I don't have any, but I like the birds too." One large corvid is resting on the lithe girl's shoulder, its head tilted to one side, signaling a warning. "We can all be friends. Sometimes they tell me secrets, and I bet they tell you too." The girl is holding several of the vivid stones between her fingers, running them over the smooth surface before she drops them into the pockets of her dress. Still, she is mute.

"Let me see what you have—they are so nice. I'd like a green stone too. You have enough of them to share." Reaching out, Pivona gently touches the girl, then draws back. Her finger is burning, and she pops it into her mouth, scowling at the salty taste.

"You don't have to be mean. I'd be happy with one stone to wear around my neck. I'll wrap it in wire. It'll look real pretty. I could do one for you too?" The girl doesn't answer but extends a hand toward Pivona's hair, gliding her finger up and down in the air but not touching the woven strands.

"You like my braids? I could do one for you too, for protection." The girl with the skin like whipped cream nods ever so slightly, shaking her long pale hair. "Sit with me. It will be easier to do." Pivona plops down on the black rock, and the girl melts next to her. She can see blue veins through her skin, she's fragile, but her scent is heavy, like wet moss.

"I'll do a small one so it will be easy for you to take out when you're ready. I used to braid the tails of my da's horses. You'll see how nice it is." The dancing girl sits motionless, gazing out into the water.

Pivona quickly separates a section of silvery hair in the back of her head, then deftly twists and twines it into a small tight braid. "There. Now we're special friends. You should give me a green rock." The girl fiddles with the braid, bringing it around to taste the loose ends of it. Reaching into her pocket, she takes out a tiny green gemstone, a pebble speckled with gold and white, then drops it into Pivona's hand. She slides away, jumping lightly down from the rock.

The black birds roost above, surveying them with narrowed eyes and beaks like scissors. Pivona joins her, clutching the stone tightly, ignoring the threatening corvids.

Turning it over in her hand, Pivona licks the dry glassy rock to bring out the colors. She's never seen anything as beautiful as the cool green stone. It's substantial, reflecting back the colors of spring. *I wouldn't have to listen to anyone's low opinions of me if I was well off. Gems like this could make me rich.*

"Maybe one more—you have so many. I want another." Three of the largest birds are perching on the rock now, inching closer to her as the ghostly girl walks backward along the shoreline, her arms raised high to the green-tinged sky. The water beneath it is black and frothy. *How strange. I wonder what's causing this?* Glancing up, Pivona is startled by the spiraling colors but is intent on owning more green stones.

Gaining ground on the girl, Pivona balls her hands into tight fists. When she strikes out. She misjudges the distance and stumbles, even though she's close enough to connect. A second blow lands hard, and the girl's fragile body dissolves into a heap onto the rugged shoreline. Moving like an experienced thief, Pivona digs deep into the girl's pockets, filling her own with the gem-like pebbles.

Her new friend doesn't fight, but several crows move in, pecking hard at Pivona's face and neck, hooking their beaks into her soft flesh. Arlen's leather protects her from the worse of the assault, but she manages to grab one of them. It flails and flaps, snapping its beak in her hands, and feathers tumble

DELEVAN HOUSE

to the sand. She wrestles with the crow trying to escape her greedy grasp. Using both hands, she wrings its neck, squeezing the life from the obsidian body, then tosses the broken bird into the water. The crumpled girl wails as it lands with a splash and sinks to the depths.

"That will teach you to mess with me." Pivona gloats, wiping the crow's blood on Arlen's jacket. The girl is curled in a ball, lying on the ground, yowling in agonizing despair. Her grief is palpable.

"Speak up! You make no sense. I gave you a chance. Don't act like I'm the bitch. Stop your racket!" Her throaty cries fill the air—a sonnet of agony, growing louder with each scream. *Someone will hear, and then I'll be blamed for causing trouble.* Pivona tries to calm the howling girl, patting her arm through the brown dress.

The wind quickens, and the sky darkens with twisting green sparks of light. "Knock off the damn caterwauling. I'm not telling you again." She smacks at the girl. Her shrieks are ear-splitting and relentless.

Panicked, Pivona puts both hands around the girl's throat, intending to shake sense into her. When this fails, she squeezes as tight, leaning forward on her knees, using her weight to silence the sounds. The girl is colorless and limp. The wailing snuffed from her throat. Pivona drags her weightless body towards the rippling waves. *If I'm lucky, she will wash out with the tide. I've done murder, and they will do away with me as well.*

Laughter echoes from a cottage on the waterline, barely visible in the mist rolling in from the sea. The crows thicken around her; their caws mimic the girl's cries.

NATASHA SINCLAIR AND RUTHANN JAGGE

A single light, low and wavering from a lantern or torch, moves closer. Hysterical now, Pivona jerks her arms from the sleeves of the jacket, tossing it over the girl's face. Her features are softer now, less apparent like those of a stone statue.

I'll go to The Rowan. Arlen will know what to do. He'll help me. Squaring her shoulders, there's no time for remorse. Pivona takes off running, her hair whipping in the wind like an ominous dark sail behind her. Catching her foot on a rock, she lands in a sprawl with one leg folded under her, bruising her pecked cheek. She scrambles to her feet, but her ankle throbs against her effort, and she resorts to limping as fast as she can in the direction of the pub.

Folks are gathered at the entrance of The Rowan. It's dark and looks closed. *That's odd. I wonder what's happening.* As Pivona drags her pained body closer, she sees Arlen standing in the middle of the tense crowd. A few men crush towards her friend, their voices harsh.

"It's you who tried to kill The Threnody, Arlen Morven. Don't deny it. Were you hoping for a taste of forbidden fruit, or are you just desperate for a roll? You'll pay dearly for this, my boy." Pivona flinches as Edgar Brown, a burly smithy known as a scrapper, lays hands on the young man, roughly binding his wrists with iron handcuffs.

"You throw your old man's fucking jacket over her like that'll hide what you did. I ran with Arlie back in the day, and he'd throttle you himself if he were still here!" An old friend of

DELEVAN HOUSE

his dad grunts, with his rough hands gripped on young Arlen's shoulders. Arlen's red head is hung low, shoulders hunched against the insults and accusations filling the air.

"What's happening? Why is Arlen in iron?" Pivona's eager to be in on the action, although her heart is racing, and she feels sick.

"A fishing boat coming into shore late found The Threnody out cold in the shallows. Looks like someone tried to kill her or, even worse, take her innocence. It's early for her to show herself, and I've got a dreadful feeling something unholy is coming. They think it was our Arlen." Arlen's cousin Heather says as she turns, noticing Pivona is bruised and wounded.

"What happened to you? There are bloody marks on your face, and you're crusty with sea sweat." Heather stops, staring closely at the disheveled girl. "Wait, did whoever did this go after you as well. What have you got there?" Her voice carries, and several women push in, shocked at Pivona's mangled appearance. She's still holding her damp undies in her hand.

"He attacked Pivona too. She's just a young girl. He needs to hang!" A woman peering over Heather's shoulder shouts. Someone bundles a warm jumper around Pivona while another goes to find the doctor.

Seeing Arlen in such distress is upsetting, but Voni knows it's him or her, and it won't be her. Not yet anyway.

"How do you know Arlen attacked... what is her name again... Threnody? I don't think I know her. Is she a local?"

"His jacket was covering her like she was rubbish. I guess he figured no one would find her after the tide came in. He's old enough to know what she is and, for the love of it all, what might happen because of him. I can't believe this is happening," the stranger who covered Pivona with the jumper says as she vigorously rubs her shoulders, trying to warm Pivona up. It's clear the drama is exciting to this woman.

Pivona's mind is spinning. She can't think straight. *I'm in the clear, but they will probably do away with Arlen over a stupid girl.*

"Let's get you inside so I can have a look at you. Those marks are swollen and turning red." John Bruce, the village doctor, is a short man later in years. He gently touches Pivona's face. She's not used to the kindness of a stranger, and her eyes fill with tears.

"Don't worry, Miss, we'll get you sorted out. I hate to see what's become of Arlen, though. I've written letters of recommendation to some fine schools on his behalf. Goes to show what you see isn't always who a person is." Pivona nods, sidling up to him. It feels good to be cared for, regardless of her guilt.

The angry crowd has swelled and continues to rage loudly as she follows Doctor Bruce, soaking in the compassionate looks of those around her.

"Unlock the door, will you, Blake?" The manager of The Rowan fumbles with a fob, then opens the door, clicking on the overhead light. "I'll be outside if you need anything, doc. It'll get ugly before it gets better tonight."

"Have a seat. I'll just be a minute. I need to clean my glasses so I can better treat your wounds. Rest, and I'll be back shortly. You're safe here." Doctor Bruce leaves the room, carefully closing the door behind him. His glasses are cloudy, but he's also hesitant to hear the details of the assault. He likes Arlen. He's sworn to tend to Pivona without judgment.

DELEVAN HOUSE

Pivona eases back in the wooden chair, steadying her breath and shaking hands. Once when she was younger, she watched the men in her family hang a man from a stout tree branch for stealing a horse. The way his legs swung, kicking, his face turning every color imaginable as he strangled to death was seared into her mind. When he was found, the authorities assumed suicide. Of course, they did. Hanging wasn't exactly legal these days. The last legal hanging in the British Isles was back in 1964. She's worried for Arlen, hoping he won't meet a similar fate, but her survival instincts are stronger than her humanity.

"Pivona McQueeney, you are a lying whore of the Devil!" The door bangs open when Minerva Morvin enters the room, then slams shut behind her. She is furious and glowers at her. Pivona shivers. "You sit there like a princess with a wee booboo while they're outside wanting to hang my boy. You will make this right, or I promise you, you'll meet a fate worse than death." Kicking the chair out from under Pivona. Minerva straddles the girl as soon as her ass hits the floor, her heavy thighs gripping tightly on either side.

"This won't stand. When the fishers brought The Threnody to us at the cottage, she was barely intact. You're not only defying the laws of man, but the more serious laws of nature that have consequences your pea-brain cannot comprehend. I won't stand for it. One of my sisters noticed the wee braid in the wilting creature's hair. No one else in this village twists hair in such a manner. YOU are responsible for harming her, and if you try to deny it, I swear they will be your last words."

Minerva's round cheeks are red, and her chest heaves as she spits in Pivona's face.

"I took you in, hoping to give you a shot at life, but no, you're too foolish. I should have known better, you come from scum, and you'll grow up even worse." Minerva hissed. Pivona tries to push her off, but the older woman significantly outweighs the fourteen-year-old. She's trapped beneath her sturdy thighs, and Minerva has no intention of letting up. "Tell the truth, Pivona, so they will let Arlen go. When I spoke with him outside, he told me he gave YOU his father's jacket because your arse was whistling in the breeze, and he didn't want you harmed. You took advantage of his kindness. I'm warning you, I may be his mother, but I am of a different mind." Minerva is wearing a pair of long scissors on a ribbon around her neck. She's seldom without them. She hesitates, then slides her fingers into the loops, snapping the blades in Pivona's face like the jaws of a starved wild animal.

"This is your last chance. Tell me what happened. Now!" Pivona can't make out the words Minerva is now muttering, eyes closed, with her head tilted upward. She doesn't realize that Minerva is cursing her soul.

"Okay, let me go, and I'll tell you." The girl's chest heaves. She's struggling to breathe. "It was an accident, I wanted the gems, and that creepy girl wouldn't share them." The door opens. John Bruce is shocked by the scene before him, but Minerva ignores him.

"Say it, Pivona. Say it! Say you're the guilty one. Arlen never touched The Threnody *or* you. Say it!"

"Okay, you fucking cow. It was me. I didn't mean to hurt her—I just wanted the stones. She wouldn't share! It was her own fault for being greedy." John's eyes are huge as he backs from the room. He needs to pass on her confession to prevent

DELEVAN HOUSE

imminent disaster. The crowd outside is loud and angry—they'll kill Arlen if he isn't quick.

Minerva is seething in hatred. She grabs the girl by her hair, slamming her head back against the floorboards. The polished blades of her scissors flash lightning silver when Minerva pinches Pivona's nose—she gasps. The enraged woman uses the tool of her trade to slice through the liar's tongue, spitting it cleanly through the middle to the back of her throat. Gurgling on her blood, Pivona splutters and passes out cold. Minerva doesn't care if she lives or dies and won't do a thing to help.

The girl's blood pools, soaking Minerva's favorite sheepskin rug—a gift from her mother-in-law on her wedding day. This only added to her rage at the pathetic gypsy by her feet.

"He's not guilty. Arlen is innocent!" Screaming until her throat is hoarse from the doorway of The Rowan, Minerva gets the attention of some in the crowd, who make way for the woman as she elbows her way to her captive son. He's on his knees in the street, with tears streaming down his handsome face, watching as two men loop a splintered rope into a noose. The villagers are high on the drama. Emotions always run intensely at this time on Badb's calendar. As if channeling the blood-lust of ancestors.

"He didn't do it! It was Pivona McQueeney who harmed The Threnody. Let my boy go!" Doctor John Bruce also speaks to the men, calm and reasoning as best he can when they're soaked in the red mist of rage.

"Minerva's right. I heard the girl say it was her. Release Arlen immediately."

Heather, and two other young women, who've known Arlen since childhood, hurry forward to wipe his face and hold him close in their arms while Edgar Brown strikes off the iron cuffs. Arlen can't stand. Minerva and the others support him, guiding him from the tense scene.

"This doesn't bode well for any of us. You don't know what's coming. The Threnody is released to the sky, but she will return, bringing the Wrath of Badb with her." Minerva spits a warning at the remaining bystanders, who turned so quickly on her son, eager for his execution. Her sewing sisters comfort the angry woman, reminding her they have work to complete before the Blue Moon. But these wise women are terrified. The future of Babd is unknown.

When she's sure her son is safely on the way home, Minerva Morvin unclenches her fist. There are three of the gem-like pebbles in her hand, plucked from the lint in Pivona's pocket. She groans as she kneels. The ordeal with the girl has caused her physical and spiritual pain. Minerva bows her head sorrowfully. She recites a prayer, using the old words, for the wounded creature, feeling the vibration of The Threnody's pain in her chest as she fingers the tiny stones.

No one would help John Bruce carry Pivona to his office. He tends to Pivona's wounds—the doctor's obligation. He's disgusted but gives her an injection for pain so he can cauterize the bleeding in her ruined mouth. She's lying on a table in The Rowan, covered with a tablecloth, moaning, with tears streaming down her cheeks. She feels no shame or guilt. *I've lost a fortune, and no one will bother with me now.*

Her situation is dire. John's words to her are harsh. "I know you can hear me, Miss McQueeney. You brought this on yourself. It's only the beginning of the price you'll pay. I'm experienced in the matters of Badb, and Minerva's justice is

DELEVAN HOUSE

deserved. No one will come to your rescue. I will provide medical care and make sure you are fed and given clean clothing, but other than that, you'll be given no comfort."

Pivona whimpers. She can't speak, and the pain in her mouth is excruciating. She tries to clasp his hand, but the doctor shakes her off.

"I'll recommend that you be held in the quarters over the library until it's time for true justice. It won't be long. Your greed and despicable actions have consequences. Minerva says The Threnody is tender and weak. If the fisher and the corvids hadn't brought her body to the cottage, we'd all be dead now. Struck down like dogs. The whole damned village. Worse, your lies and conniving almost cost a good boy his life. I'm afraid there will be no forgiving you, Pivona. You might want to show humility, say your words to whatever high powers your people believe in, and ask them for mercy."

Pivona's mind is pain slicked, but she grasps the seriousness of her situation. She decides to sleep, believing everything will be well once she can explain. The girl doesn't realize she will speak words with a forked tongue that no one will listen to.

Arlen's at the sink in the small kitchen, carefully wiping the stains from his beloved leather jacket. He's using an old toothbrush to scrub the seams, thinking about how cool his father was. When satisfied, Arlen pulls it on over a black tee shirt, then tucks his wallet in the back pocket of his worn jeans.

Sighing, he heads to the back garden, where his mother sits stitching in the early light.

Arlen's been dreading this day. It's here sooner than he planned because of last night's events. The conversation he needs to have with Minerva will be hard.

"Mum, thanks for looking in on me last night, and I appreciate the tea. It helped me sleep." Minerva smiles up at the handsome young man. He's the image of his father. "I'm leaving Badb. Now. Today. I've packed a few things, and I hope it's okay if I leave the rest here for a while? Just until I get settled and can sort out school and a job."

Minerva bites her lower lip hard. She's been expecting this, but she's still raw. Blood swells to the surface, and she forces herself to let go before she breaks the skin.

"Before you start crying or trying to stop me, please understand that I love you. You're my best girl, mum. It's always been you and me, especially since Dad. I'm not leaving to hurt you. I just can't stay here one more hour. I won't face the pity or those who still might believe, somewhere in their small mind, that I am guilty. That I would do such a thing. I won't suffer the gossip or the fools. I've got enough money for a while and can check my outstanding school applications on my phone. The signal's better everywhere else anyway."

Minerva nods, setting the green cotton she's stitching off to one side.

"You're right. There's no future for you in Badb, you don't have the hands of a smithy, and farming is damn hard work for little reward. Where you sleeping tonight—do you have a plan in place until you find somewhere to settle?"

DELEVAN HOUSE

"Yes. I'm going to stay at a friend's in Inverness. Then go from there once I know what's happening with school. I'm still hoping to get into Glasgow or Edinburgh. It'll be an adventure, mum."

"You will, son. I know you'll make all your dreams happen. I've always said you can do anything you put your mind and heart to, my Arlen. You make me so proud. And I know your dad would be too," Minerva's voice shook. "Promise you'll call me every day, no matter what time. I have affairs to settle, and this isn't over. I promise that one way or another, some who live in this wretched village will not forget their treatment of my son."

"I know, mum, but I'm leaving last night's nightmare behind. I'm leaving all of this behind, except you. Everything will be better soon." Arlen holds out his hand to help his mother up from her chair. Minerva wraps her arms around her tall son, breathing in the smell of him and a hint of her beloved husband still embedded in the leather. Tentatively rubbing his back, she tucks a small cotton pouch into his pocket with her other hand. Releasing Arlen, he gives her a knowing look, placing his hand over the pocket. Minerva's eyes become glassy with more tears welling to the surface.

"I'll be safe."

She reached for his neck, "Time to go. Before I start crying and you feel bad. I'll be fine, the sisters have work to finish before the moon, and we'll cover you with protection." Minerva's voice wobbles. Arlen nods, gently removing her arms from around his neck.

"I've got a taxi waiting. We'll talk soon, mum. I love you." Slinging his heavy backpack over one shoulder, Arlen winks, then heads from the garden.

Minerva's hands are shaking when she sits back down, but she knows her boy will be okay. She's relieved he's leaving. Very few do. There's no place for his kind in the darkness of Babd. She'll call up the sisters tonight, and together they'll convene.

They must prepare for Samhain.

Badb Karma

Caoimhe gives short history lessons on the area as they drive through winding country roads toward Badb. Jenna enjoys taking in the views—everywhere is so green. Between naked autumnal trees, evergreens rise like giants and veins of water splice through the land. Jenna is aware of subtle but unusual changes, noticing that many road and place signs are in a language other than English. She considers asking her guide but decides she doesn't want to come across as ignorant. Jenna already feels intimidated by the woman beside her, so she leaves it as a subject for another time.

"Is this your first time over here, then?" Caoimhe isn't much for small talk, but she has learned that it can be beneficial. It takes effort for her to engage in small pleasantries.

"Yes. I've always meant to come for a holiday but never really had the chance until now."

"Why here? I mean, it's a pretty dreich wee country. Are you an Outlander fan or did you see Braveheart as a kid or something?"

Jenna chuckles. "Oh, yes. The film with an American actor fulfilling the romanticized ideal of a brave and noble Scotsman filmed in Ireland. Sure." She rolls her eyes playfully.

"You laugh, but it may surprise you how many Americans were suddenly laying claim to Scots ancestry based on a wildly inaccurate bit of fan fiction."

"I get it. I am a bit of a history buff, or at least I was when I was at school. It's a historically inspired fantasy, nothing more. It brought in the big cinematic bucks, though! I'm sure it helped inspire tourism over here, right?"

"That it is. And yes, but that has its ups and downs. I'm sure you can imagine," Caoimhe raised her perfectly arched brows, winking at Jenna. "So, why Scotland then? Is it a historical interest that got you hopping the pond over?"

"I suppose it was my grandmother when I really think about it."

"Ahh, the old ancestry then. Is she from here? McCray is your surname, right?"

"No, nothing like that. As far as I'm aware, there's no Scottish blood in the family. She used to tell me stories from here when I was a kid is all."

"Stories, huh? What sort of stories?"

"The scary ones about water horses who drowned children. Redcaps murdering unsuspecting tourists exploring castle ruins. Tales of forbidden love between selkies and humans, myths about faeries and some about the painted people." Jenna smiles at the fond memory.

"No Scottish blood, but your surname has roots somewhere here. McCray..." Caoimhe pauses thoughtfully, rolling the name over her lips. She looks like she's searching her mind as her gaze travels over the broken road disappearing beneath the windshield. "How are you spelling it? Is it M A C C R E A?"

"No. I'm M C C R A Y. Perhaps there is something in there from way back when, but my family is somewhat disconnected, shall we say, so I wouldn't know. I've never really thought about it." Jenna regards the other woman curiously.

"I understand that. My family has their... *secrets*, too. Well, it's a known name here. I am certain that the original form was MacRaith. We actually have some MacRaiths around these parts. Who knows, maybe you have long-lost family here."

"Maybe. Wouldn't that be a story."

"So, if it wasn't family, was your grandmother a folklorist?"

"She just liked to tell tales. Stories that no one else knew, perhaps. It was probably what made me love history and turned me into a bookworm."

"Well, that is never a bad thing. Growing up, I spent many hours in my mother's library. It's full of dusty old volumes. Some would be extremely hard to come by these days." This piqued Jenna's interest in her new friend of hers. There was definitely more to her than met the eye.

"That sounds magical. We didn't really have books at home growing up. I had to find my own. Perhaps I could have a look at your mother's collection if it's not too much trouble?"

Caoimhe smiles, though there's something uncomfortably feral in how she displays her white teeth. It sends a chill through Jenna.

"Perhaps," Caoimhe says, turning her attention back to the road.

Increasing speed, Caoimhe drives too fast over the rough country roads. The bouncing adds to the surreal effect of the view for Jenna, who's clutching the black leather seat. *I guess I'm lucky to have someone willing to show me around. It certainly takes my mind off Layton.*

NATASHA SINCLAIR AND RUTHANN JAGGE

Random herds of sheep and a few highland cows line the way on the narrowing road, funneling them into the village. Caoimhe dodges them expertly, her sight fixed on the cluster of buildings in the distance.

"What is that horrible stench?" Jenna covers her nose and mouth with her hand. The air is sharp with salt and fish, but there's something else, causing her eyes to water profusely.

"Not a country girl, are you." Caoimhe is amused.

"No, it's not that. It's something else. It's noxious and acrid like a burning landfill—nauseating." She gagged, covering her mouth with the sleeve of her jacket.

"It's just the forges, you know, where the iron is worked. Badb is all about the ore." Caoimhe is oblivious to the stark change in the air. "I guess I'm used to it. I grew up in a house with water on three sides, between the two lochs and the North Sea. The water diffuses the sulfur from the mines to some extent. It won't bother you much after a day or so."

Jenna swallows hard, trying to suppress the bile crawling up her throat.

"How long do you plan to stick around? It's not like I need to be anywhere, but I'm not sure life in the country is for me. I appreciate you, but I need to formulate a plan too. I can't bounce around without at least an idea of what to do next." Jenna is slightly uncomfortable. She's not used to the undivided attention this beautiful person lavishes on her. Caoimhe laughs, patting her new friend's hand. Every touch, even innocent, seems infused with flirtation. Jenna has no interest in women, but this one intrigues her.

"You can and should. There's a lot to see and learn around here, but I predict Badb will suit you. It's unique, like nowhere

DELEVAN HOUSE

you've experienced. There's an event in a couple of days, a family reunion of sorts. I'm bringing you as my plus one. In the meantime, I'll introduce you around, and we can catch up on the local gossip. The village is ALL about the gossip." Caoimhe smirks. *I still smell Grant on you. I intend to find out exactly how and why I was betrayed. Then someone will pay.*

Jenna wipes at the window, admiring the rows of simple cottages. Badb isn't exactly picturesque, but the natural features make it interesting. Holding her breath as she cracks the window open, Jenna breathes in the aromatic harvest of the surrounding fields. *That's better.*

Caoimhe slows the car to a crawl, gliding it through the small village, eventually parking in front of The Rowan, where a few men are talking outside.

The day is calm and cool. There's not much activity apart from the few folks outside the pub. Jenna senses the group of men staring hard when Caoimhe opens her door.

"Come on, don't be shy. There are a couple of rooms above the pub, and they're aware that I'm visiting. Don't expect much. It's a hangout for the working boys, but this place is pretty much the center of the universe here." The stares turn to chillier glares as the men quickly disperse. Only one of them moves towards the car.

"Will you be needing a hand?" Denny Patterson is a stout and compact local with ruddy, pockmarked skin and wispy hair pulled back under a tammy. Jenna notices he doesn't make eye contact, uncomfortably shifting his weight from side to side.

"Hello. No, we're traveling light." Caoimhe brushes past, causing him to trip aside as if startled. He rubs hard at his arm when a corner of her embroidered shawl makes contact.

Tipping his hat, he scrambles down a gravel path leading to the shore.

Jenna nervously steps inside. The pub's dining room is warm, and the food smells delicious, but her shoulders stiffen under the chic jacket when the conversations of the men having lunch grow quiet. A few of the younger ones grin broadly at the pair of beautiful young women. Others avert their eyes, paying closer attention to their plates.

"They won't bite, but I'll bite harder if they do." Caoimhe's entrance sucks the air from the room. Every curve is displayed in her green dress, but her aristocratic features harden as she surveys the men. Her nostrils flare, and her alluring eyes narrow when she spots Grant and Robert deep in conversation at a small table under the stairs.

No time like the present—I might as well let him know that I know.

Caoimhe eases between the worn tables in their direction, but Jenna grabs her from behind, gently pulling her back. A girl carrying a tray comes through the kitchen door, but she stops dead in her tracks and then retreats. A confrontation is brewing.

Fuckity fuck fuck fuck. It's HIM!

Jenna audibly gasps when she recognizes the blacksmith, confirming what Caoimhe already knows. "Oh, look who's here. Shall we say hello?" Caoimhe teases Jenna, but her expression is cold.

"Can we go upstairs? I'm kind of tired and would like a shower or at least a wash." Jenna is trying hard not to panic as she whispers, bowing her head into Caoimhe's hair to avoid the look on Grant's face when he notices them.

DELEVAN HOUSE

He doesn't look happy.

"It can wait. I want to say hello to my old friend." Shrugging Jenna off, she paces over to the table.

Robert finishes his beer, then reaches across the table and slugs down the remaining draft in Grant's glass. "Grant, I don't know how you can drink this alcohol-free stuff. It's nothin' but piss water," he huffs. "I'll get them in." As Robert swivels to stand, he stops in his tracks. His eyes run up the legs of two women approaching their table. "Who the...." His sentence ends abruptly. Robert knows everyone in town. They all do. And outsiders never come this far into the village, at least not unnoticed, and never for long. But women who look like these two are rare. Robert is baffled. When his eyes finally pause on *hers* of blazing green. He knows. He'd never be able to explain how since he convinced himself that Grant was making her up as a crazy figment of his imagination. But it was *her*. *Those eyes are mental.* The women came towards them, stopping near the table by Grant.

"Caoimhe?" Robert stands, holding out his hand to greet the glamorous intruder. "Well, fuck me sideways. You're actually real."

She ignores him. Her eyes bore into Grant's head, waiting for him to acknowledge her.

Grant turns.

"What the f—." Caoimhe strokes his hair and then holds his chin as she moves in for a hello kiss. She traces his scar slowly with a finger. Grant jerks out of her grasp like he'd been jolted by an electric current. His scar was usually numb, but now it throbbed. He turned his attention to Jenna, which made him feel grounded. He was conflicted by Caoimhe's sudden presence and wasn't sure the feeling was good after all this time.

"I will say it's nice to see you again, but I'm wondering why you're here with this one?" Grant stares at Jenna, trying to hold himself steady. His mind is reeling.

Jenna's cheeks are hot. *Nothing I say will be right. What have I walked into?*

"Ummmm... we're friends. She invited me here for a family event." Jenna notices that Caoimhe is digging her tapered, rouge fingernails into the side of Grant's neck. They look longer than before. There's nothing friendly in the look Caoimhe is giving her.

"A family event, you don't say." Grant spits the words back at Jenna. And yanks Caoimhe's possessive grip from his neck. "I suggest you go back to Anand, or anywhere else for that matter. There's nothing here worth hanging around for. In fact, I'll drive you myself. I have work to finish at the forge, but we can leave in a couple of hours. I'm more than willing, so say yes." Grant's standing now, with his back to Caoimhe. He's amused at Jenna's discomfort. Entertained that his offer to the flustered young woman has briefly removed his panic. *No good could ever come of an introduction of any kind to Lady Delevan. I have to save her.* He won't have this innocent woman infused into their traditions in any way. *Why did she have to show up now?*

"She's staying here for the time being. I have plans for us. You're sweet to offer. I suggest you head back to your fires, but I want to speak with you later—alone." Caoimhe's annoyed, and her features are more angular than before. Her fair complexion flushes deeper, and her eyes are flinty-green slits.

DELEVAN HOUSE

Nightmares flash in Grant's mind: This perfect woman was eviscerated while her body rode his. Her mouth on his nipples, licking his skin. The way they laughed together. Then blood and screams. Lust. Love. Horror. He's trying to present a brave face.

"I cannot imagine why you'd show up out of the blue like this. You've no idea what you put me through. And bringing her here, an outsider. You know what's coming. Maybe you're like your mother," Grant's lip curls with disgust. Caoimhe is unimpressed.

Robert puts an arm around Caoimhe as if to lead her away. He's trying his luck, but she's not having it and swats at him. *How dare you stand up for this girl. A basic human. I'll not only take her from you, but I'll do a lot more if you don't play nice.* Her jealousy rises to a fever. She forces herself to suppress a growl with great difficulty. The air around her is brimming with static.

The bar is unusually quiet. Rather than attracting a crowd, as would normally happen with a conflict in the village, patrons cleared out fast.

The quiet is unsettling.

"Damn you." Robert flinches, drawing back his hand. There are three long red scratches on it. He licks at them, crunching his face with concern.

"Is there someone I can see about a room?" To diffuse the tension, Jenna looks around the empty space, gathering up a handful of Caoimhe's shawl. Caoimhe yanks her wrap away and pets the fabric, smoothing it without looking up at Jenna, like a hurt animal.

Jenna's voice is calm and direct. This is more drama than she needs. Even though Grant is amazing, she now understands that the pair have a history between them—one that's very much unfinished.

"Caoimhe, thanks so much for all you've shared with me. I appreciate you, but I have money and can take care of myself from here. I'll find my own ride in the morning. That way, you can stay and enjoy time with your people." She's unsure of Caoimhe's motives now. Something in her attitude has changed. She's too predictable.

I'm going to listen to my gut. It's telling me to get the hell out of here.

"We're done here." Caoimhe is fuming, rivulets of spittle are forming at the corners of her mouth, but Grant refuses to back down."

"Why don't you tell your friend about our little family gathering under the light of the moon. You're so fucking obvious and out of line by using her to bait me, and I'm not playing whatever game this is." Grant wraps his arms protectively around Jenna. Caoimhe's glare cuts daggers through them both. Jenna wiggles away, barely avoiding the open-handed slap that lands on his scarred face. "I'll give you this one, Caoimhe. You don't want to do it again." Grant looks huge, standing next to the furious woman wrapping the shawl tightly around herself for protection.

"I know what makes you tick, and I'll stop your clock." Caoimhe snaps.

"Look. I don't know what's happening here, but I have my own problems. It's been nice knowing you." Wanting no part in the violence, Jenna inches away from the pair towards Robert, standing quietly near the door. Either he's amused by the show or too drunk to involve himself effectively. He's wise to stand back—for a change.

A stocky woman with gray hair blocks Jenna's exit.

"It's getting late, Miss, and you won't be finding a ride at this time. Grant's in no position to offer. He has pressing responsibilities, don't you, Grant?" Her voice echoes in The Rowan, sounding more like a command than a question. Caoimhe has pulled herself away from the handsome man. She's sitting at the table he previously shared with Robert, composing herself.

"I've been expecting Miss Delevan, so there's a room ready upstairs. We'll get you sorted out with transportation early in the morning. I'll speak to Cook first thing. He'll know someone trustworthy. Caoimhe? You'll stay with me tonight, and that's not an invitation." Caoimhe scowls at the woman. Her voice is calm but deadly and calculated, like right before disaster strikes.

"I'm weary of this, Minerva. You have no power over me or what I choose to do. She seduced Grant. He's been with her, and I will not abide such disrespect. I won't stay with you, but I promise you, everything will be different tomorrow. You'd be wise to waddle back to your dank cave before I decide to include you in the festivities. I may not be able to outwit you, but I know who is, and so do you. Now fuck off!"

Robert backs away as Caoimhe struts out the door, easing into the darkness.

Minerva remains calm at the fiery young woman's threat, unphased by the dramatics of the evening. Caoimhe's insults are unpleasant, but as a landlady, she deals with her fair share of drama. It comes with the territory. As far as love and jealousy are concerned, tensions often flare, especially with first lovers. Minerva takes none of it personally. She shakes her head but keeps her composure.

Grant wonders how familiar Caoimhe and Minerva are and why Minerva never let him know that she was okay. Before she disappeared almost seven years ago, Caoimhe didn't claim to know her. He'd had enough for tonight. His nerves were on end. With the ritual looming, he needed to rest.

"I'm sorry you're the pawn in her game, Jenna. This is my fault. I should have known better. You're wonderful, and I wish I could know you better. You'll be safe here tonight. Minerva will make sure of it." Grant bends, then grazes her cheek with a kiss. Jenna knows it's goodbye. He does as well. His life doesn't allow him to live normally with a woman like Jenna, an outsider.

Another one bites the dust. I have awful luck with men. Jenna shrugs it off. She decides to keep to herself from now on.

Robert is standing outside, watching the sky shift and blend shades of green into marble. He and Grant leave, disappearing into the dark.

Climbing the stairs behind Minerva, Jenna's legs are heavy with exhaustion. The hallway at the top of the landing is stuffy with fried onions and salt. Jenna unzips the borrowed jacket, exposing the stolen necklace as she takes it off. Minerva stiffens, then coughs loudly. She covers her mouth with both hands, muffling a scream. It's like taking a bullet to her eye. *How in the hell did she get it? No wonder Caoimhe turned up here with her.*

"I have some things I borrowed from Caoimhe. I'll leave them behind for you to return them to her." Minerva nods but doesn't take her attention away from the pendant. Her body is tense, but she tries to conceal her unease from the stranger. "Will she be okay? I mean, I didn't know. How was I to know?" Minerva barely hears Jenna's voice. She's rattled to her core.

She clears her throat.

"I'll brew a pot of tea and leave it outside the door for you. It's my own blend, and you'll rest well." Minerva turns on her heel, heading back down the stairs. Jenna watches her. *The woman moves well for someone who's no longer young. There's something to their country folks. Maybe it's the air.* She's miserable to be alone in yet another small and strange room. However, this one feels more alive than the room in Anand. The carpet is red and patterned with gold fleur-de-lis. The furnishings are simple but elegant, including a fine gold-framed antique mirror. In the middle of the room, piled high with pillows, a carved wood bed is dressed in fine cotton sheets in a rich shade of deeper burgundy red. There's also another fabulous hand-stitched coverlet on the bed. *The seamstress*. She remembers.

It's stifling. Jenna assumes from the heat of the pub below and the drama. She sighs, then crosses the room to shift the heavy curtains. Jenna tries to open the small window, but it's sealed shut. Layers of crusty magnolia paint cover the sill. She huffs and strips off the borrowed jacket. The door opens, and a tray with a pot of steaming tea and some fruit scones slides in. "This will settle you down for a decent rest. I'll not come in. I have downstairs to close up." Minerva's head is at the crack of the opening.

Why is everyone so damn awkward all of a sudden? Jenna is exasperated. She wishes she had stayed in Inverness and simply booked a hotel. *How did I end up wrapped up in some small-town drama?* Her head is thumping, and her eyes are heavy.

"Thanks." The door slams shut before she has the chance to say anything else. Jenna hears the tumblers click. *What the fuck? Why would she lock the door?* Too tired to fret about it, she decides it's for her safety in this weird little place.

Jenna strips to her underwear and brings the tea tray over to the bed.

Locked in from the outside, with nothing to do but worry. Physical exhaustion and one sip of the landlady's brew knocks her out cold, and she slept without dreams haunting her rest.

Once in a Blue Moon

Once every seven years, on Samhain, all village residents must participate in the ritual without exception. They have no choice but to obey the instructions set over three hundred years prior, in 1667, by the town's magistrate, Lawrence Gordon. Lawrence held steadfast and ensured the village's survival by keeping their demon locked down. He vowed to keep Badb safe and righteous. Even in death, he saw to their continued security, embedding laws firmly in Badb traditions. Deviation from tradition was not an option.

Kings, queens, and governments came and went, but the rules decreed by those authorities didn't matter in Badb. They were written for frivolous, weak heathens who had lost their way, and Badb would not falter under the eye of the Gordons.

Every village member received a personal summons—the young and old, all are equal in their duty. Folded papers are left on every doorstep. Only the village committee knows what the sigils, carefully drawn inside each sealed envelope, represent:

Resident of Badb,

Your village needs you. This Samhain sees the seven, and we are each required to obey. We are bound to our ancestors by blood, God and oath. All are commanded to meet at the village hall no later than 10pm. Our duty is set in blood and stone.

NATASHA SINCLAIR AND RUTHANN JAGGE

The distinctive structure of the village hall was built at the crossroads of Badb, south of St Magnus Church and the village school. In its earliest form, it was a clock tower. No building was ever to be built higher than the clock overlooking Badb. This was written in their bylaws and is adhered to—aside from the forges.

The tower isn't especially imposing, but rather it looms stout. The village hall was expanded little by little over hundreds of years. Expert craftsmen used the reclaimed wood of lost ships that crashed onto the shore over the centuries. Heavy wide boards, worn smooth by water, are stacked high and round, joints packed tightly with mortar.

Folks say that if you press your ear against particular points, you can hear the crash of waves or the wails of a desperate drowning man. The hall is surrounded by the intricate decorative lacings of Sutherland ironwork fencing. An elegant round moon gate, painstakingly shaped from the mahogany staves of a great hull, decorates the entrance. The hall sits empty unless there is a marriage ceremony or a mass for a newly departed soul.

Minerva Morvin and, until recently, Pivona Mc Queeny cleaned the hall monthly. Polishing the wooden benches, lining the chamber inside with warm beeswax mixed with turpentine, and checking for any cracks in need of repair. The construction around the original clock tower was completed in 1902. They held an abundance of secrets and stories; if walls could speak, these would scream.

DELEVAN HOUSE

There's no formal jail in Badb, as criminal events are rare and dealt with swiftly with unwavering discipline. From the small window of a locked room on the upper floor of the village library across the street, Jenna watches as first a few, then a growing line of people winds snake-like through the narrow streets. Robed and almost void of individual identity, they slither slowly toward the hall.

The silence of their procession is eerie. *What are they doing?* There's no talk that she can hear as she strains at the glass. Even the forges are quiet—with no fires or fresh smoke pumping into the night air. Only the constant stink of Babd's smog hangs in the atmosphere.

Jenna is currently detained for questioning in a makeshift holding room. At least, that's what she was told when she awoke groggy in this strange little room. *What the hell is wrong with these people?* All she intended to do was get away from Layton and start over. Scotland was nothing like she imagined.

Shivering, Jenna pulls her thin wrap tighter, wiping at the foggy glass dripping with condensation. She wonders about the ominous gathering crowd. Cold terror crawls up her back. Even her teeth ache as she considers her predicament. Unconsciously, she reaches to fidget with the necklace she's been wearing since she stole it from her ex, then remembers it's not there. *I should never have trusted Caoimhe.*

Since finding herself in this room, Jenna's hazy memory flashes random glimpses of Caoimhe conversing with the landlady from the bar, Minerva. But she has no memory of their conversation. She did recall that it ended with Caoimhe leaning over her, removing the green pendant, then kissing her on the mouth. Jenna shivers, uncomfortable with the memory of how the strangely alluring woman's lips felt on hers. *I still feel her.*

Down the hall, in a smaller room, Pivona McQueeny wipes her nose on her sleeve between whimpers. She knows all too well what the crowd's mood is and that her fate for harming The Therondy, a respected being, is sealed. Her mind races.

There may be an opportunity to escape, or even better, the voters will consider my contributions to the village and lowly status when sentencing is decided. I wanted nothing more than to be one of them and fit in. To be a part of Badb.

Pivona McQueeny stayed behind in the village—her family left and neglected to return for her. She was an abandoned young girl desperate to survive. She'd welcome sympathy if it saved her, and she'd gladly play the victim. From her days of snooping, earwigging and gossip, she knows that this is a night of uncompromising ritual tradition, full of respect for ancient papers and long-dead men. It's also the time when wrongdoing is judged. She believes herself to be way ahead in the game and is confident in her ability to charm. She is wrong.

Pivona hasn't eaten anything but a watery, over-salted porridge in days. Her wounded tongue throbs constantly. Her entire face and throat burn. Bits of the rough oaty grains get caught in the wound. She hates feeling trapped; it's in her nature to be constantly on the move. Travellers believe they should never stop moving.

DELEVAN HOUSE

Watching as bright leaves drop from the trees surrounding the building, Pivona wonders if they scream before they land on the ground. *Do they also know their lives are almost at an end?* She blames her unfortunate situation on those *fucking birds. They saw what I did.*

They see everything.

The villagers arrive. Each member of every family residing in Badb is dressed in ceremonial robes delivered alongside their summons. The robes are uniform. The ankle-length heavy green cotton fabric is lined in red with long cuffed sleeves. Deep hoods hide their faces, draping around their tense shoulders. They are handmade for each villager for this occasion by Minerva Morven and her sewing circle. Stitched into each vestment, in a pocket on the left breast, is a handmade rowan cross tied together in crimson-dyed twine. The dye is made from the blood of the tree's berries mixed with water from Delevan Loch. This talisman is carried to keep each individual safe from the wrath of any witch on this night.

Most of the villagers are somber, befitting the occasion. They are full of dread, but there's also a tickle of excitement for a few who would never admit it. Minerva Morven checks off the arrivals, then closes the heavy doors once every villager is accounted for.

With this signal, Robert Lawrence strolls to the pulpit. He stumbles on his robe but catches himself.

"He's been on it again," whispers Heather to her brother, Cameron. He towers over her, tall like their cousin, Arlen. They have a strong family resemblance, and Cameron is often mistaken for Arlen's twin. This often happened while working at The Rowan together. He shakes his head in agreement, keeping his eyes on the front of the hall.

"Aunt Minerva kicked him out of the pub last night. He was making a right arse of himself."

She huffs. "He's a Gordon, though, right. They think they're untouchable." She rolls her eyes, unable to conceal her contempt.

"Mhmm," Cameron tightens his lips in agreement. The mic squawks as Robert Gordon takes the stand.

"As we gather, on this night for the seven and blessing of three, to bind our fierce foe, I beseech the villagers of Babd, the wise and the new, to walk the path of our ancestors. A path laid out along ley lines of the land which bore us, feeds us, keeps us. We shall hang our heads and remember those who have sacrificed for us. We will gather the sacred stones and be blessed by the presence of the pure one who walks between worlds. Our angel and our curse, The Threnody. We shall honor her selection of the three. With our hands over our left breast." Gordon places his hand over the rowan cross hidden beneath the fabric, and everyone in the room mirrors the action.

In chorus, "Rowan tree and red thread make the witches tyne their speed. Rowan tree and red thread make the witches tyne their speed. Rowan tree and red thread make the witches tyne their speed.

Robert continued. "We summon protection in the seven with hearts of loyal dedication and pure intention. We persevere and preserve our way, as protected by our ancestors. We honor them in our ritual. Tonight, we keep the witch bound!"

Six villagers emerge from the crowd and stand in formation by the pulpit. Robert steps down and joins them. Leaning over, he fumbles at the neck of his robe, extracting an ornate iron key hung from a thick belcher chain. With it, he opens a hatch on the floor. Another man carefully sets the hatch door on the floor, so it doesn't slam.

They are each handed a lit lantern and proceed to enter the chamber beneath the hall. The line of robed figures disappears into the pit.

A few minutes later, they emerge, one by one. First, Grant Sutherland clutching a small box. The small round rowan-wood box holds the unusual *key* required to unlock the ingredients for the ritual. The precious contents will be handed to The Threnody. The Edge-Walker is the only being who can read the divine instructions scored into the sacred green stones, using the long-lost language of the painted people, the Picts.

Robert had assigned four of the burliest villagers to retrieve the outsiders, Pivona McQueeney and Jenna McCray, from across the street. His younger brother, Marcus, eager to move up the Gordon ranks, was to fetch the American girl with the assistance of Rodger McDonald. The other two, Kieran Campbell and Denny Patterson, who work under Grant Sutherland, are charged to collect the gypsy girl and bring them to the ritual site. Their signal to proceed is the closing of the hatch.

NATASHA SINCLAIR AND RUTHANN JAGGE

The solemn walk to the ritual site is led by the Gordon family, as always. At the helm is Robert Lawrence Gordon, alongside his longest friend, the village's leading blacksmith Grant Sutherland.

Grant edges closer to Rob, sensing that the line of villagers behind them are too absorbed in conversation and speculation to hear them.

"Do you think it will include the young this time?" he whispers.

Robert pauses, kicking black rocks out of the way. His heart isn't in the proceedings. He prefers to celebrate Samhain by staying up late, feasting on delicious food, sharing ancestors' stories around a fire, and drinking. Lots of drinking. Now, they demand that he personally presides over an event that will result in someone he knows meeting a terrible fate. Every seven years. They seemed to come faster now that this burden was on his shoulders.

"No telling, but I have a bad feeling. Too many things have been happening lately that don't feel right to me," Robert mutters cautiously.

Grant nods. He agrees with Robert's instincts. They've been friends since they were bairns fishing together with their fathers and attending the village school. They are as close as brothers. Robert cups his hand around his torch. He's now shoulder-to-shoulder with his friend.

DELEVAN HOUSE

"You're right. This time feels different, and I don't think things will be the same after tonight. I don't like it." Grant's voice is unsteady.

"You're just shaken up from yesterday." Robert doesn't fully understand the hold that love can have on a person.

Grant exhales with a tense sigh. "I hate my family's responsibility in all this. The darkness to our craft for the sake of this damned binding. Of course, I do it. But I just feel that I'm done with it all. You know?"

"It's a heavy thing to carry, my man." Robert looks around uncomfortably, hoping for something to end the conversation. He's not in the mood. He needs to focus and get on with the task before them. Then he can go home to relax and have a drink. His mouth is dry, his heart is racing, and vomit threatens to crawl up his throat from his cramping stomach. He needs a stiff drink to stop the hangover from kicking in, and he's confident that the hair of the dog will set him straight again.

"It is, but you know what will happen if even the slightest mistake is made. My family didn't ask for this, but they stepped up and were the only craftsmen with enough old ore and skills to forge the blackest iron when the situation turned to shit. One misstep and the Sutherlands will be as hated as the *witch*." Grant whistles softly through his teeth. "We'll no longer be the keepers of the bind, and part of me is terrified of what that might mean."

Ahh, fuck. Here we go. Why does he think he's so fucking special? Like any of us asked for this. Fucks sake. Robert's head is starting to throb.

A pair of older men gain on them, offering a swig from a flask of spirits. Grant holds one hand up, politely declining the offer, but Robert obliges, swallowing deeply before handing it back to the larger man, who is frowning at the pair.

"Ur ye too guid then tae share a wee swally, Sutherland? Ye could use a bit mair fur oan yer chin, like that huge fuckin' cat wi' the steely claws we saw the ither nicht." He elbows the shorter man by his side, who's gulping from the dented metal flask. Leaking whisky from the corners of his mouth. He wags his head up and down, confirming the sighting. Trying to maintain his composure, Grant flashes a grin.

"You didn't see a cat. It was the booze clouding your vision." Grant tuts shaking his head at the drunk.

"It wis that despicable Delevan creature. A'm tellin' ye. We saw it plain as day, right?" He elbows the other man again, who spits his whisky out, swiping at his chin with a forearm. The green sleeve of the robe darkens from his slobbering.

"It wis the fuckin' cat, right enough, we were at the edge of the trees, lookin' fur mushies tae sell tae Minerva, 'n' it came at us oot a naewaur, A tell ye. I cannae git they horrible green peepers oot ma heed, havnae slept since." He grabs Robert's arm tightly for emphasis, steadying himself.

"It's a bad omen. Anythin' tae dae wi' that damned hoose, any beast associated wi' it, is why life disnae go easy oan us here. And why ma Missus left me. The time is comin', though. A'll have that cat's heed mounted o'er ma mantlepiece before the next turn o' the wheel." Both men laugh, their torches flickering in time with their noise.

"I'll wager there's no cat. I'm with Grant. Don't be making things worse than they are, and stop with the whisky. We'll all need clear heads for what's to come." Robert and Grant quicken their pace, leaving the other two to chat with anyone who'll listen regarding their sighting of an elusive Delevan shapeshifter. Robert regrets not relieving the men of their flask.

"Auld fools. They've been in at the auld witch-finder stories again. This ritual just gets them too damn riled up. As if we've not got enough to contend with." Robert laughs.

Grant had seen the cat skulking in the shadows. His first sighting of it was five years ago. The black specter, darker than the night, emanating a white flash of light from its chest. And those haunting green emeralds, like in his nightmares and dreams of... *her*. His mind had gone there before, but it wasn't logical, and he flicked it away like a bug. *But, after last night...* he shook it off again. *This is not the time.* Even as a resident of the superstitious village of Badb, he always endeavors to be logical.

"I really don't know how you can keep leading this as you do," whispered Grant, leaning in towards Robert's ear again. Robert sighed deeply. He's missing the interruption of the old fools.

"Same as you, mate. We don't exactly have a choice in the matter."

"Says who, though? I mean, it's high time we make a change. No one wants to do any of this. Not again. The last blue moon still haunts me."

Why is he such a pussy? Robert grows impatient.

"It's how we've always done it. I'll say it one last time. We don't have a choice. It was written, and we have to maintain the binds. You know this."

"Do I though? Let's be honest with ourselves. No one really knows for sure what will happen if we don't. We have bloody old writings to go by and nothing else. Those and the damn stones."

"Grant, it's not worth the risk, mate. Let it go."

"But any one of us is at risk? It could be you tonight, or it might be your sister."

"I swear, brother. This is the same damn conversation as seven years ago."

"I say it's time we make our mark, Rob. Change things. If we don't, maybe no one will."

"It's not like you don't believe, Grant. We've all seen her. Hell, it's not even about only her. *Them*. Those eyes of hers that are always watching. Then, there's The Thren..."

"Right, okay, I know, I know. Don't. Don't even say her damn name. That one gives me the heebie-jeebies." Grant shivers.

"Have you seen her yet?" Rob asks.

"Nope. Not since what happened with the gypsy girl."

"She'll be there. She always is. She has to be. Minerva's group will make sure all is properly in place, including the Edge-Walker."

"Yeah. But I'm fed up with it. We are outcasts to the world. We're not even on any of the maps, you know. We're like Scotland's dirty wee secret. Plus, maybe the Edge-Walker won't be ready, Rob. I mean, no one has tried to wring The Threnody's neck before!" Grant spits. Even her name makes his blood run cold.

"The Threnody will show. I can't imagine what would happen if she didn't. And to the other point, perhaps we are the outcasts, but it's not much better out there either. Have you watched the news lately? I wouldn't want to be part of any of that. There's plenty of good reasons to keep doing what we do."

"Maybe. Still, I think about what it would be like to leave all this and have more. The idea runs through my mind sometimes, you know?"

"Ever since, Caoimhe, you mean?" Robert raised his eyebrow, turning to his friend with a smirk.

"I miss her, man."

"Even after that bloody display last night?" Grant didn't answer. "You're obsessed."

"Maybe, but you would be too. If you had spent time with her. I can't shake her voice from my head. Her smell, the feel of her skin. There's no one like her."

"Calm down, Grant. Now is not the time to be giving yourself a hard-on." Robert smacks his friend hard on the back, laughing.

"Uch, be quiet. I just miss what we had. Or what I thought we had,"

"You love her."

"Yeah, I do."

"Maybe, she'll come back for good. Everyone always does if they are from this place."

"It's been almost seven years. It was shortly after the last ritual that she left. That's the longest anyone has been gone from here."

"You came back," Robert said.

"Yeah, when I thought she was... Well. I don't know what I thought anymore. Plus, last night. I wonder if I ever really knew her at all."

NATASHA SINCLAIR AND RUTHANN JAGGE

Tears pooled in Grant's sad blue eyes. He's glad it's dark. He had never been in love before, nor did he imagine he'd ever feel the same again about anyone other than the girl from Delevan House. His mind wandered through the women he'd been with since her. They were fun, but none of them came close to Caoimhe. He was spellbound, and he knew it. Grant didn't care; he still wanted her.

The villagers cross the slippery mud-caked duckboards between the serpent and the crow, carrying their burning torches—it always had to be living flames heralding their arrival. Some of the younger generations protested—why not use the battery-operated torches? But they would not risk diluting the traditions with technology.

This was no time for trial and error; the old ways were the only way.

Even the summons were hand-delivered on paper and black ink and not transmitted through waves that could be intercepted, exactly as their ancestors wrote and executed.

Badb's déjà vu in sevens. Nothing would take the place of a living flame, and the procession is the same now as it always had been.

These are the same families who rallied for the failed execution of their village witch. Their ancestors were present for her binding to the house and them.

Bloodlines carried histories that could not be vanquished, and the ceremony, right down to the vestments they

DELEVAN HOUSE

wore—made by Minerva Morven, whose mother was the seamstress before her. Like all lines in Badb, responsibility stretched backward in an unbreakable thread.

Cloudy ghosts smoke the sky. Wisping grays stretch across the blackness, heightening anticipation. The ancestors are watching as the veil thins on this night, bringing the dead closer to the living. The ether presses in from the elements.

They could all feel it—fear, dread, excitement—it prickled and scraped at their skin under the heavy robes. It could be any one of them.

She stood at the top window in the spire that looked over the house's main entrance. The Lady in Green. Her aura cloaks her, and the apparition shimmers. Younger villagers heard the vivid stories of this specter, but she *is* real. They weren't just stories. She *is* here, standing over them. Lady Delevan is their captive prisoner. A witch who could not be vanquished.

When she was captured in irons in 1667, she was pricked by the magistrate himself. Every cavity of her body was searched for the mark. The villagers knew what she was, but formal proceedings were followed to ensure no mistakes were made in her condemnation.

Grueling interrogations lasted for ten days, and she was kept in a dank, dark hole within the bowels of the Clocktower. She was starved, beaten, and refused even a drop of water. The so-called witch never made a sound, not one whimper. Although her mute response to pricking was a sure sign of a witch, Lenore Delevan's silence infuriated Lawrence Gordon. His sadism rose with her quietness.

On the night of her execution, she was dragged from the hole and tarred—refusing to scream even as the burning pitch poured over her, destroying her remaining beauty as it seared through her flesh. They forced her mangled body, once flawless, now scarred and shredded roughly into a barrel. Her torturers and neighbors rolled the drum through the village. The cracking sounds of her bones breaking could be heard as they laughed sadistically, and the eager villagers cheered her terrible fate.

Lady Delevan was not granted the mercy of strangulation. She would not admit to her crimes, even with the evidence stacked against her. In truth, Lawrence Gordon preferred it when the accused would not confess their treasons to God or their devilish affiliations. While he enjoyed legally throttling a filthy heathen whore, he yearned for the sounds they made and the look in their eyes as they burned to death. The stench of burning witch-flesh on his shirt and the sound of their agonizing screams made him burn with desire. Tugging furiously at his rod was his post-execution ritual. His big finish.

There was to be no mercy for the Delevan witch at his hands. She was sentenced to be burned alive, and Lawrence Gordon was feverish with anticipation. The pyre was built, and she was restrained to the stake. The entire village bore witness; no one was too young or infirm to miss their witch's burning. Lawrence Gordon threw his torch into the pyre first, then the village elders followed. Fire engulfed the mound of wood, cut especially for the occasion from the forests of Badb. Heat and

DELEVAN HOUSE

excitement rose in unison. Lady Lenore Delevan's body, thick with tar, was caught in her inescapable fate.

The heat caused the onlookers to step back. The ravenous fire rose rapidly towards their witch, spitting sparks of orange into the inky night.

...

...

Badb's witch would not burn.

Even though the devices used against her were severe, Lady Lenore Delevan's power wasn't weakened enough to eliminate her from the natural world and send her back to the Devil. Perhaps even he didn't want her in his Hell.

Instead of engulfing her, the flames licked around her tarred and broken feet, never touching her skin. The residents of Badb had to devise an alternative method of binding their witch, and they did.

After temporarily trapping her in specially forged iron bracelets molded to her forearms, Lawrence Gordon relied on his beliefs to outwit the dark arts and bind their demon that could not be defeated. He saw this burden on his village as another test from his God, and he would not fail in his mission. Even if it meant unthinkable sacrifices to the villagers; it was their duty for the greater good.

History can be inaccurate, and the only records of Badb's history were written and approved by only one man. Lawrence Gordon. He made his word and religious fanaticism their history. It survived unchallenged.

Now, in 2020, some want to challenge the archaic traditions.

Arriving on the grounds with everything in place, ensuring that the binding ritual of Badb will continue to hold its monster captive.

A fresh log, painstakingly hollowed and oblong in shape, waits on the pebbled bank of the Badb Loch. The air is thick with a mist reeking of rotten fruit instead of the usual combination of ore and sea salt.

It's the scent of decaying life.

It is the scent of death.

Several women in Minerva's sewing circle, wearing simple black dresses and separate green hoods designed to match the villagers' robes, wait for the procession to reach the bank. They are tending the traditional Fire of Badb, started hours ago by Grant Sutherland and the blacksmiths who feed the forges and make ready a ladle to carry the molten ore.

Two of the women see to The Threnody, who sits motionless on one of the black rocks. Her body is lean and pared to the bone, with skin as translucent as the white gown covering her. Thin fingers massage three black pebbles plucked from the bank relentlessly in precise circular motions, wearing them smooth with focus and intention. The women are not comforted by her meditation.

They gently bathe her with warm water from the two lochs, heated over a small fire, then infused with salts. They brush her

DELEVAN HOUSE

silvery hair and anoint her slight body with oils of the rowan and yew. She's been under their care since Pivona left her in the shallows for dead. Although she hasn't made a sound since her injuries, the women hear her desperation; her soul cries, and these empaths feel her celestial agony. Not one of the women dares to glance at the shadowy figure positioned on the slate roof, looming high above Delevan House. The Threnody stares in its direction, unflinching. The flock grows larger, moving in a formation circling the stone structure. The moon rises like a spotlight on a tragedy unfolding below.

As the inky sky intensifies and clouds shift into the distant horizon, the residents of Babd take their places, anxious for the proceedings to begin. A cerulean halo takes shape around the moon, and the unearthly glow heightens sensations. The air is sharp with static. The villagers of Badb feel this seduction intensely. Many are light-headed and queasy. Residents who've survived this ritual before harshly remind the uninitiated of its purpose and theirs.

The fierce pull of a rare Samhain Blue Moon is amplified by the power of the dreadful apparition longing for release. When the silhouette of the Lady of Delevan House raises her hands, commanding the man on this moon to do her bidding, everything changes.

Everything....

Fractured prisms of light reflecting in the stained-glass windows of Delevan House shoot vivid rainbow daggers into the stygian sky, piercing its mantle.

The heavens crack.

Several villagers drop to their knees, covering their heads with their hands, whispering incantations in the old tongue.

The portal is opening.

"You are ready, precious." One of the women, dressed in black, helps The Threnody from the rock, wrapping her arms around the waif protectively, gently hugging her fragile form a final time. She kisses her cheek, feeling nothing beneath her lips. The Threnody is more ghostly than she usually is during a binding. The woman then walks to her place near the blazing fire, where her sewing sisters stand in a circle. Two of the other women reach for Anthea MacRaith's hands in a gesture of love as she takes her place among her sisters. Her twelve-year-old daughter drowned a few years earlier, and the recent incident with The Threnody has struck her heart and soul heavily.

Minerva is with them, and their exclusive position away from the others is unchallenged. Her circle stands nearer the soft lapping of the crow than the horror of the house the others gather around. The Threnody floats boneless like a child specter, and her bare feet leave no imprint as she makes her way to Robert Gordon.

He's standing anxiously next to Grant Sunderland, who's shifting his weight from side to side, uncomfortable and refusing to make eye contact with anyone. It's not like him to appear nervous, and his dour mood is unusual.

"This is the last time, Rob. I'm leaving Badb for good tomorrow. The prescribed Coldiron is ready as it must be, but I won't be responsible for preparing it anymore. The only way to stop this pageant of insanity and murder is if one of us makes it happen. We have to break the cycle. I'd rather leave without her and take my chances alone and with nothing than stay here. This is outdated and ignorant bullshit." Grant's voice is low, but his teeth click in anger.

DELEVAN HOUSE

"I've had enough of your crap! You can't leave. I won't let you. I don't like it either, but this is who we are. Nothing will change." Robert's eyes are narrow and furious. It's all he can do not to shove Grant to the ground in front of everyone. "Why now? Huh? Are you so pussy-whipped that you think blood oaths are meaningless? Don't make it about you. Don't make me hate you, my friend, and do not underestimate me." Robert kicks at Grant's ankle with the toe of his boot, smirking when his friend winces. "I thought all your talk about leaving was noise until now, but you need to get a grip, or I will." Robert elbows Grant hard as he shoves past him, moving further away to where Jenna and Pivona are gagged and bound together wrist and ankle by short iron chains.

Caoimhe Delevan stands solitary, ankle-deep in the cold water, watching the aurora taking shape. Quiet ripples are beginning to form, but something in her stance gives the distinct impression that she sees more than anyone else. Steadily, the dynamic aurora fills the sky with violent waves of beauty, like capillary waves on the surface of a vast body of water. With each ripple and lap, the sky dances—green, amber and hues of lighter blues break through the cracks. The waves overhead are a mesmerizing magick.

"Hello, Mother. I know you're waiting." Caoimhe feels Lady Delevan's power in the pendant clasped tightly in her hand. The green stone mirrors the color spilling from the sky, pulsing like the life force of Delevan House. She dips to cool the heat of the metal, dripping the water over her head—cleansing herself in anticipation. The weighty stone twists as she holds it up from the water. The back of the pendant glows with a marking that wasn't visible before. A turned-down crescent and V-rod overlay. It pulses like a brand scored into the metal with fire. The freshwater from the loch sizzles against the mark, and drifts of steam rise in the air in the same branded impression. Caoimhe recognizes the symbol. She's seen it in the house and inside her mother's books, but she doesn't know what it means. Her curiosity is piqued, but she slides it to the back of her mind for another time. Tonight is too important for her thoughts to be elsewhere.

"We must begin. Mark the three." Robert bows low to The Threnody, the wee slip of a girl, standing before him with outstretched hands.

The villagers stand quietly, with bowed heads, none daring to glance at the ethereal creature. Robert's hands tremble when he hands her the green ritual stones, etched with markings and symbols of the Picts, like those surrounding Delevan House.

The Threnody nods her acceptance weakly, bringing the stones close to her face. Her eyes close as she inhales deeply, pulling their message into herself. Only the fire crackles in conversation; the others are silent.

Jenna's eyes are wide with fear, but Pivona struggles with the chains, yanking and pulling. She's viciously whipping her head from side to side, trying to dislodge the gag. *She's not human, but I know what she is. I know of her magick. Let me speak!*

"You're guilty of harming The Threnody, and I suggest you show some respect. Your judgment is coming," Robert sneers and grabs Pivona by the back of her neck, forcing her to watch as The Threnody makes her way to the shallows, surrounded by her guardians, the crows. Pivona feels no apprehension or humility. She's jealous of The Threnody again, missing the gossip the birds once shared with her. Or perhaps, she only imagined they did. She is filled with hate and bitterness for them, too—*feathered fuckers! Traitors!*

They move in synchronicity, darting and swooping. The crows mimic The Threnody's strange and solitary dance, and the shape of her body changes like liquid with each step of her ballet. The Edge-Walker arches her back with willowy arms raised high as she offers her being to the brilliant green and purple heavens above. Dozens of black wings flap in approval, but the villagers are resigned and watch with a collective silence.

"Wait for her song, you little wretch." Robert jerks Pivona's chain hard. He wants her gone for good. She's a worthless nuisance. He secretly hoped her Traveller family would come looking for her so he could force them to pay Badb a hefty restitution for the girl's many petty crimes, but it didn't happen.

Pivona whimpers, but her demeanor is defiant.

The Threnody kneels, tossing the stones gently on the ground in front of her. The fire illuminates her actions as if in slow motion, flames flickering as her hands move patiently in circles around them. A single crow rests on her thin, bowed back, watching intently as she works. It's Fraoch. Lady Delevan's crow. When the girl is satisfied with the message of the stones, she moves quickly to the apprehensive villagers waiting anxiously for the result. Many are desperate to be back in the safety of their hearths, and all are deathly afraid of being chosen. Her paper skin is the palest blue, with deep veins lining her forehead like an unfinished sketch. She frowns, furrowing her brow as she lays a stone in front of three.

Pivona McQueeney. Jenna McCray. Cameron Morven.

NATASHA SINCLAIR AND RUTHANN JAGGE

One for the blood. One for the iron. One for the soul.

Caoimhe's eyes widen when The Threnody places the stone in front of Jenna. Cameron is the only one of the three who understands the meaning of the vivid green stone at their feet.

Grant's throat is dry, and he's choking back tears. He's fond of the Morven family and understands the immense grief that they have already endured. But he has no choice. The Sutherland family are bound not only by the iron they forge but by an oath. This ritual of Badb is his duty. The lives and future of the village depend on the strength of his character.

The residents mutter approval as the group walks towards the fire. Flames rise in praise of the waving aurora illuminating the heavens.

Those who are present bear witness and understand what must be done—relieved to have no part in the proceedings.

Minerva Morvin stares uncomfortably at the green stone by Pivona's feet. She feels responsible for the unruly girl despite her actions. Minerva's lesson to the girl's foul tongue should have been enough, and she pushes back a tinge of guilt. Her breath catches in her throat when she sees the green stone at her nephew Cameron's feet. Her desperate whimper brings tears to the eyes of her nearest sewing sisters. Minerva clutches the handsome young man's arms tightly, leaning her head into his shoulder.

"My darling boy. You are the best of us. We will love you, always." Cameron clings tearfully to his Aunt Minerva. He's aware that there's no alternative. The stone has been placed by the Edge-Walker. He refuses the berries she tries to press into his hand.

DELEVAN HOUSE

"Give them to the girls, aunt. I'll be ok. Promise. Please don't cry for me. I ask only that you don't allow anyone else to suffer after this night." Gossips claim that Cameron is sensitive, preferring the company of books, music and rare species of plants to the attention of several young ladies, who lust after him. But at this moment, he has the strength of the gods in Minerva's eyes, and she is proud of her brave Morven nephew.

"Robert Gordon, remove those gags. Even though they're chosen, these girls still have a voice." Minerva glares at him. "It's no wonder no one will have you. Women don't ever deserve such treatment." Minerva cannot conceal her distaste for the Gordon boy. She's always viewed his family as trouble, even if they are at the top of the village hierarchy by default of the past.

Caoimhe laughs when Robert pulls the cloth from between Jenna's teeth. Her laugh is like a screeching gaggle of geese, high-pitched and ear-splitting.

"As it should be—filthy, lying thief!" Caoimhe hisses at Jenna.

Robert's face is hard; something in him is changing. His authority is no longer benevolent. He's out for blood.

"The selection makes sense to me," Robert says. Caoimhe grabs Jenna, kissing her roughly, invading her dry mouth with her tongue. She pulls back, then runs her tongue slowly and seductively up the girl's cheek. "Too bad we won't have the chance to enjoy each other and Grant together." She laughs with a horrendous, ugly squawk again before sliding away into the night, barely visible in the crowd.

"What does this mean? Why is this happening? Please talk to me, Grant!" Jenna calls out, but Grant Sutherland doesn't look back or acknowledge her plea.

He has a plan and needs to be ready.

"Listen to me Pivona." Minerva stands nose to nose with the whimpering girl. "Take these, and don't say a word." Robert is watching but knows better than to challenge Minerva when she slips yew berry seeds into the girl's clenched hand. "You'll know when. Chew them slowly, then swallow quickly. I'm sorry I didn't do more." Then, she repeats this action with Jenna. "Find a way to chew and swallow these. They will ease your struggle." Inhaling sharply, Minerva touches her forehead with three fingers, then hurries away with her hand over her heart. This night is almost more than she can bear.

"Enough. The Threnody is waiting; her presence is thinning. It's time."

"No. Please, it's hard to breathe." Jenna wrestles away as Robert replaces the gag. Pivona tries to bite his hand, like a wild animal, snapping and thrashing, but her wounded tongue hurts too much. Her entire gullet feels swollen. Every movement of her face amplifies the agony, reminding her of her penalty. She bites her tongue accidentally and lets out a desperate pain-filled shriek. Tears flow down her cheeks. Robert yanks the chain, dragging the terrified females to the crowd on the bank.

The Threnody stands alone, a solitary figure at the water's edge watching Delevan House. Lady Delevan is more visible, absorbing the energy of the cursed village. Crystalline tears streak The Threnody's face. Her sadness is palpable. The birds return to their roosts around the eves and arches of Delevan House. Even those who normally roost on the small island in the center of the loch gather atop the majestic structure.

DELEVAN HOUSE

The sky cracks like a bullwhip strengthening the aurora's effect, and the birds take to the air in formation once again. They surround their mistress and the dark figure of the massive stone gargoyle she caresses like a lover.

The lightning arcs. It bends, mimicking the curves of the ironwork fence surrounding the house. Ancient, unquiet historical magicks stir.

From the flickering flames below to the sky above, deep cerulean light cascades, covering Delevan House like a bridal veil. Gasps ripple through the crowd as they watch The Green Lady.

Hanging above them is the glorious and rare spectacle of the Samhain Blue Moon. The color intensifies, and splashes of white energy, like orphan stars, twinkle madly. The superstitious villagers believe that this glorious aurora borealis signifies their binding is divinely blessed.

Badb is entirely silent. Even the crows stand to attention. Once again, the winged demons become statues scattered and resting atop Delevan's vaults.

There are stories of the first binding and how it took place under a rare Blue Moon. They had not seen another moon like it again since their catalog of sevens began—until now.

The impact of this phenomenon was not foretold. There was no history to compare it with.

The recipe for Lady Delevan's chaotic and failed execution and entrapment many moons ago may be the key to her freedom. The key to the undoing of Badb.

NATASHA SINCLAIR AND RUTHANN JAGGE

Minerva and her circle are not pleased by the spectacle; something in this binding feels wrong. Minerva also longs for change in the traditions of Badb.

The women cluster together, unwilling to participate in the process any more than is necessary by their mandatory presence. Usually, they would say special incantations and bless the offerings, but not this time. Minerva leads the whispering women in a chant of protection.

"Is everything ready?" Robert is still dragging Pivona and Jenna when he approaches Grant, giving final instructions to Edgar Brown, the smithy tending the ladle at the communal fire. He needs the Sutherland Coldiron to be perfect. The girls are still kicking against their chains. Their faces are red from straining and crying, and both are caked in thick mud. They have wild hair, torn clothing, and their legs are grass-stained and bloody.

"Yes. Listen close, Rob. This is it. I don't care what happens to Badb or anyone else after tonight. If I can find the stomach to pull this off one last time, I swear I'll never do it again." Beads of sweat cover Grant's chiseled face.

"You've grown soft, my friend. Be glad it's not a wee one or an elder. They're just outcasts, not even one of us. Be thankful, you miserable cunt. You've done and seen worse, so don't threaten me. There's no way you're leaving. This is who the fuck we are. I won't allow it. Do your damn job." Robert Gordon's clenched jaw twitches. His patience for what should be a

DELEVAN HOUSE

straightforward process is short, and he's been drinking since breakfast.

The Threnody is more fragile than ever, but the success of the binding ceremony relies on her song. The fae creature continues scratching sigils into the earth, oblivious to the villagers: Crescent. Shield. Maze.

These graceful movements stop when she begins to twirl faster and faster. Several of the village women bow their heads and clutch each other's hands until their knuckles are white. Parents cover their children's faces in desperate attempts to preserve their innocence, and others avert their eyes in fear.

Stretching her arms to the infinite depths of the radiant sky, The Threnody yawns open her thin lips to sing her sacred ode to the spirits buried in the walls of Delevan House and those that reside in the cosmic waves of the Merry Dancers.

The villagers hold their breath.

Waiting.

Praying.

Nothing.

There is no sound.

The ache of silence.

The Threnody's sacred song does not break free from her ghostly mouth.

Her throat is too damaged, and her once-angelic voice is silenced because of Pivona.

The Threnody closes her lips, folds her arms around herself, and hunches. The villagers watch in strained silence. The waiting creates terror in their hearts. Many have the same thought; *the death of her song is the death of us all.*

The Threnody unfolds her body, reaches upwards again, and opens her mouth to sing, but what comes out is only a throaty croak.

The notes shatter like broken glass.

Flat.

Dead.

A blanket of darkness coats the sky, and the smell of molten iron tears at the villagers' eyes. The Threnody doesn't cough like the others as the haze thickens, but her pitiful wailing fills the night. She sounds like a wounded animal begging for release. The crows cry for her as she eases onto a rock, wrapping her arms tightly around her pointed knees.

Minerva shudders, speaking in low tones to the women close to her. Her sharp intuition is on high alert.

"Sisters. We will go to ground. Hurry, she's coming." While the rest of Badb stare at the spectacle above, Minerva Morvin and her sewing circle disappear into the gloom under cover of their black gowns. Their robes may bear Minerva's protective design, but her wrath knows no bounds.

"The Coldiron won't hold temperature if we wait much longer," Edgar elbows Grant. "I don't like the feel of this."

"Steady man. I promise I won't ask this of you again," Grant assures him. Edgar rolls up the sleeves of his shirt, shaking his head. Grant trusts him, there is respect between the men, and he knows the truth.

"It's time." Resigned to the task, Grant bows his head to hide tears of frustration as Robert addresses the villagers.

"Badb. This is our oath and our future," his voice booms into the night, echoing against the silence and the crackling flames. "The three are chosen by The Threnody. Pivona

DELEVAN HOUSE

McQueeney will be executed for her crime of attempted murder against The Threnody. She is the blood. Cameron Morven has been chosen for the soul of Badb. We will offer Jenna McCray for the iron. She will become a guardian of the realms between land and water. Her life force will join the others in iron, binding the monster to her walls." Most in the crowd murmur approval. When some younger residents try to protest, parents sharply remind them what is at stake.

Children, who don't yet understand the situation, poke at the fire with sticks, unaware of how serious the binding is.

Jenna is frozen, numb with terror and unable to feel her fingers. Nerve endings in her body fire at full pelt, and she feels a sudden surge of determination. The prisoner pushes against her terror and strains forward. She thrashes, shoving hard against Robert. His sour whisky breath hits her in the face when he laughs.

"Get your hell-bitch off my hands, Grant." Jenna stumbles when Robert shoves her away hard. Grant wraps a protective arm around her, but his touch is firm, not reassuring. Nothing like when they had been together.

"I'm sorry, I really am. Forgive me or curse me for eternity. I'm already damned." Grant's eyes glisten. He's as helpless as Jenna. Caoimhe's watching his every move, and she blazes with hatred when he tenderly brushes Jenna's hair away from her face, then kisses her forehead. "Take the seeds Minerva gave you when I lay you down. I'll wait until they kick in. You will feel numb, not pain. I promise to make this quick." Her face is wet with tears and snot. He's vulnerable and childlike in his grief. Grant knocks the lock open on the chains around her ankles with a single hammer blow. Grant supports Jenna. They take several unsteady steps together. None of the villagers move to help or hinder him.

"Please. What did I do? Help me fix this. I thought she was a friend. I don't know why I'm here," Jenna sniffles pathetically and slumps against Grant, but his focus is on the wooden frame they're moving towards.

"Nothing. You've done nothing. Wrong place, wrong day. In another life, I might love you in spite of her." Placing his strong hands on her shoulders, Grant gently forces Jenna to her knees. Her eyes are pools of desperation and confusion, and Grant almost caves. *She is the last one,* he reminds himself, steeling his composure.

"Chew and swallow the seeds," he insists. Jenna looks at the crushed, revolting mess in her hand. Grant nods as she pushes them into her mouth, wincing at their tartness. She retches but manages to swallow. The poison rapidly takes effect, slowing Jenna's heartbeat and dulling her mind.

Easing the young, condemned woman down onto her back inside the hollow log harvested from Badb Wood, Grant fights the urge to run. Glancing around, some women are weeping as they finger worn beads. Others refuse eye contact, staring at the ground. Most Badb men are stoic, but a few wipe tears away. Their compassion for Jenna, a stranger, is evident. Some of Robert's cronies leer, clapping him on the shoulder in approval. *Sadistic fucks,* Grant thinks.

Jenna's breathing is irregular, and her eyes are closed. "Pour without hesitation. I won't have another innocent suffer." Moving clear, Grant motions for Edgar and another smith to open the ladle of molten Coldiron. Edgar tilts the vessel,

DELEVAN HOUSE

turning the release valve. The stench of Sunderland iron covers the crowd standing under the grim sky.

Thick, steaming ore floods Jenna's body, and within seconds, only a shining slab of black rests where she lies. One brave woman steps forward, tossing wildflowers onto the viscous grave. When it cools, the slab will be placed alongside the others in waters by Delevan House, ensuring that Lady Delevan remains bound.

When the binding was created, no margin was left as a possible escape by Lenore Delevan or the village. Whether Lawrence Gordon intended it or not, he imprisoned them all. It was well-documented that certain witches had the power to manipulate the elements, including water. Ever since the North Berwick witch trials in 1590, which spanned two years and were fuelled by those who conspired to kill King James and Anne of Denmark by raising storms and wielding the power of the seas to capsize their vessels—witches and water were not trusted. One slip and she could reign terror on them all. So, the villagers controlled their lochs by lining them with iron-encased sacrifices as guardians. As far as Badb was concerned, this method ensured that no demons of the waters could come to the witch's aid. And the imprisoned Lady Delevan could not use it to manipulate the water or wield the element as a means of escape.

Without fresh Sunderland iron, the succubus would devastate the village with her profane need for nourishment, and it would cease to be. Everything had to be executed precisely as written in the ancestral texts detailing the ritual.

Caoimhe slithers to Grant's side, eager to comfort him. He slaps her away, flaring her anger, "I should claw your eyes out." Caoimhe raises her curved fingers, then stops. Her face contorts with rage. She knows jealousy is beneath her, but she can barely control herself.

"NO! IT ISN'T POSSIBLE!" Robert is frantic. His arms windmill the air as he watches Jenna McCray, covered with iron ore, rise up, with her body still burning. Her features are barely recognizable, but she wipes the fluid metal from her face as easily as if it were mud. Jenna is in shock; her movements are choppy, and she's unable to speak beneath the grip of the yew's poison.

"What have you done to us, Sutherland?" Robert pummels Grant's chest, screaming at his friend. "Did you taint the iron? The bind won't hold. This is a death sentence for us all!" He screams.

"I warned you. I'm done with all of this and you. It's torture and murder in the name of some bloody myth. Playing on the fear of what might happen if we don't obey our damn ancestors. They're dead, for fuck's sake. There are reasons the witchcraft act was repealed, Rob. 1736 changed everywhere else in the country, but here in this miserable village, we ignore history! It's obscene! All of this shit! It's fucked, and I am done. You'll have to figure it out on your own from now on." Grant shoves Robert back, intending to leave. *To hell with you all.*

But Robert grabs the hook hanging from the iron ladle and swings it with the full force of his weight, sinking the tool deep into Grant's neck. The shocked villagers, frozen by the spectacle, finally react, screaming accusations at each other as the nightmare unfolds.

Blood sprays from Grant's neck, covering the dripping iron and Jenna in a spray of pumping hot arterial blood.

DELEVAN HOUSE

"I'm sorry," gurgling a final apology to a catatonic Jenna, Grant Sutherland's strong body hits the ground. His steaming life force continues to pump from his corpse, seeping into the earth. His dead eyes hold onto the view of stars forever.

Caoimhe tumbles to the ground next to his body, and her hysterical keening draws the attention of The Lady in Green as the damned figure comes to light.

"MOTHER... MOTHER..." Caoimhe is lying on top of Grant, sobbing and screeching. "I *want* him back. I *need* him. Bring him back to me!" She is inconsolable, caressing her dead lover's body.

Two villagers try to help Jenna to stand upright. Grant is greatly admired by most of the community. Jenna's skin is torn, with solid veins of metal embedded in the wounds, but there is no blood. The molten iron striped the skin, preserving her form. She is a breathing sculpture, seared alive as if covered in burning tar, only with deeper wounds. Jenna McCray, the living metal sarcophagus, stares ahead with lifeless eyes. She's too heavy for the women of the village to move as the iron slowly solidifies, so they stand by her side instead.

"For the blood! For the blood!" Rob Gordon commands attention, holding his arms high with authority, justifying his heinous act. *He had it coming. Who was he to endanger Badb with his arrogance? His idiotic ideas! Like some woke fool!*

A young girl, no more than six-years-old standing in the middle of the panicking crowd, points at the sky. It's changing again. The inky sky ripples in black waves.

They are not clouds.

The swarming black *clouds* move in unison, honking shrilly and incessantly. The sound is loud enough to wake the dead and make the living cry out in torment. The residents are in various degrees of shock and grief. Some openly weep, and others are silent. The stench of hell isn't worse than the steam covering the crowd. It's a dense metallic fog infused with the smell of burning meat.

Edgar Brown is on his knees, beating his chest and tearing at his hair, refusing to believe a good man, his mentor, and loyal friend is gone. Heather Morven and several other young women who loved Grant wail their relentless mourning, propping each other up in support. Rob Gordon is surrounded by men who support his boorish posturing, some from loyalty, others out of ignorance. He's still clutching Pivona's chains as if she's a prize possession, but the fight is gone in her young body. She's limp with exhaustion, no longer conspiring to escape.

The parts of Jenna McCray, still intact, rest mutely on the cold ground. Someone has draped a garment over her head and shoulders, but her face is a ruined mess of flesh, and her gaze an emotionless abyss. Caoimhe's bent over Grant, cradling and kissing his face. She laps greedily at his blood, comforting herself as she absorbs the loss of her partner. *He'll be part of me forever. He will live within me.* Suddenly, her back stiffens, and her animal instincts sharpen to high alert.

Run. Hide. Death is coming.

Her acute hearing picks up the honking sounds of geese flying in wedges so dense their formation is solid before anyone else understands what's coming.

And for a change, the Delevan daughter is terrified.

Caoimhe gently eases Grant's body from her lap onto the ground, then making herself as small as possible, she subtly moves to the outer edge of the clustering villagers. Without

DELEVAN HOUSE

calling attention to herself, she shifts into predator mode. Under the moon, her metamorphosis is less excruciating than on other days. Her human body turns itself inside out. Her pale skin splits into a grotesque zipper, tearing down her middle. Bloody gore and viscera splat to the pebbled lochside, painting the stones red. She emerges as a large lustrous feline, the rumored creature humans fear—the cat-sìth.

Stretching out her large paws and sleek back, Caoimhe slinks towards the rock that The Threnody's tiny body drapes over. There's almost nothing left of the sprite, but her small weak hand gently strokes the smooth head of the black cat, comforting them both. They feel the impending doom.

The Daughter of Frenzy nears.

The stunned residents of Badb watch as large stones drop from the splitting sky onto the surface of the snake—Delevan Loch. Water transforms to solid mass as the rocks hit the surface, expanding and magnifying the ancient duckwalk that rides between the two lochs, linking the village to Delevan House.

The iron fencing surrounding Delevan House buckles and sways, threatening to snap from the power pulsing through the air.

The Lady of the House is no longer visible; there's a deep, broad layer of stealth protection around it and her, provided by the teeming masses of crows. They are no match for a Stealer of Souls, The Bone Mother.

A supernatural fire floods the sky, replacing the glorious shifting greens and blues of the borealis with a fierce burning torrent. These malignant flames herald the arrival of she who draws the veil, claiming souls for her court while casting offending mortals headlong into an abyss of eternal torment. Nicnevin, Queen of the Unseelie.

Roused from her peace, she is angry at the collective failure of the village of Badb to honor their oath. Grant Sunderland's decision to contaminate the Coldiron has consequences.

"Is it now raining rocks too?" Heather and her friends huddle together, dodging bruises as murky rubble, some the size of footballs, thud to the ground.

"It's the birds! It's the monster's birds!" Doctor John Bruce shields a young boy, wrapping him tightly in his arms. The villagers scatter. Crows plummet to earth by the dozens, tumbling from their roosts, unable to fly or signal imminent danger to the others. The ground rumbles as the trees of Badb Wood shake. The Threnody's shrill screams of agony are more dreadful than the disaster unfolding. She feels the life-essence of every corvid like a fatal blow to her heart.

The Threnody is near extinction when the exquisite Goddess, Nicnevin, appears, hovering in the sky above the Edge-Walker. The Dark Queen wears flowing garments of every shade of blue that send infinite sparks into the night as she moves. Her beauty is exceptional, but another face lies under the flawless surface, one worn heavy by an eternity of wisdom and judgment.

The Goddess effortlessly plucks the dying Threnody from the land below. The weak fae creature is drawn up through the air until she reaches Nicnevin, who cradles her in her ethereal arms like an infant, weeping as she examines her. The Threnody is one of the most precious beings under her protection. When Nicnevin realizes the extent of her injuries, her screams put out the flames of the Fire of Badb. The lochs and the North

DELEVAN HOUSE

Sea beyond the cliff face roll their creatures onto the land in crashing waves. The force of her wrath causes her image to twist into tattered-gray rags. Her repulsive visage screeches with grief. An applewood wand, covered with shards of human bone and peridot gemstones, guides her descent to the earth, accompanied by her soldiers and minions of torment.

"Run! She'll kill us all!" Older villagers try to hobble away, stumbling and crying, but their families hold them back.

"Hold! Stay where you are, don't leave. If we end this now, we are doomed for eternity. We must beg for our lives and all that we are, or we will fear something much worse. I will petition the Goddess for mercy. My family's legacy demands it!" Pulling himself up to full height and raising his voice above the crowd, Robert is suddenly sober as he petitions his people. Pivona's chain wraps around one hand, but he raises the other fist in a greeting to the spectacle of the heavens. No one is ready for what appears behind the skeins of geese.

Morphing between her forms, Nicnevin's shape alternates between incredible radiance and hideous crone as she appears, surrounded by the Unseelie's most gruesome creatures—The Sluagh na marbh.

Trembling, Robert drops to his knees in front of the apparition. Pivona is forced to crouch next to him like a feral and defiant mutt. She's managed to work the gag from her mouth. Bending quickly, she picks up a fallen crow with her butchered mouth, holding the bird's body firmly between her teeth. She struggles to keep her swollen, forked tongue from touching it. The girl's tormented mind slides out of place, grasping for sanity, for escape.

NATASHA SINCLAIR AND RUTHANN JAGGE

Maybe she'll think I'm one of them and won't be able to see me. I'll hide behind this one. I will become. Pivona imagines pine feathers erupting from her skin in rippling waves, then bursting into a jet cloak. She pictures herself as one with the flock, rising in the air, weightless and without chains.

Most of Badb are on their knees or prone, with their foreheads touching the spongy ground, except for Jenna, still facing skyward in her metal cocoon.

Who is responsible for harming The Threnody? Nicnevin's voice penetrates every mind, a divine invasion slithering into each psyche. It flutters like the wings of a night moth, defying her fierce appearance. *I demand to know who did this to her.*

One of her Wild Hunt horde stands by The Unseelie Queen's right side. A nine-foot-tall male dressed in black chainmail tenderly cradles the body of the sweet clairaudient being. She's barely a feather in his bulky arms. Bulky gray tentacles whip out from his legs instead of feet. The villagers tremble in silence. *Her summons did not seek my approval. Her song was a desperate plea for help. I will not ask again.*

The Sluagh are restless, each repulsive, and all are eager to maim and slaughter the villagers at her slightest command.

"Goddess. Pivona McQueeney harmed The Threnody." Robert Gordon can barely speak and dares not make eye contact with Nicnevin. Two of her Sluagh are now by his side; they are skittish and ready to kill him. They look like misshapen twin goblins. Their bodies are bulbous, shiny, gray lumps with heads almost the same size as their bodies. Their terrifying mouths were like Payara—both have the same long razor teeth. Rob could see his reflection staring back at him from each three-eyed monstrosity.

DELEVAN HOUSE

Move, damn it, or we're all dead. Robert wills the hand holding Pivona's shackles to rattle the chain, signaling her as the culprit. Another of the demonic beings, with sharp iron spikes for teeth, removes the crow from Pivona's mouth. Its hands are crab-like pincers. The monster nips her hard on the cheek with its rusty teeth, pulling away a chuck of flesh. She howls as the creature swallows a piece of her. Her mouth, once again, fills with blood.

Waves lap against the banks of Badb Loch. From the depths, a colossal white beast gallops and rears from the water, landing its' gigantic hooves on the shore. The ground beneath shudders. Its physique is foreboding and muscular. It exudes strength, beauty and immense danger. Most are busy fixated or dare not glance at the Unseelie Queen and her ghastly demons from the sky; they don't register when the water horse breaks land. This beast is almost twice the size of a fully-grown Clydesdale. The Kelpie snaps onto the garment of one of Heather Morven's friends, dragging the screaming girl towards the water, intending to eviscerate and drown her. It stops dead, releasing the girl with a snarl when the Goddess speaks.

Remove her restraints. Now!

Edgar Brown crawls on his belly, with his chin in the dirt, to Pivona. He strikes off the cuffs from her ankles and the chain securing her wrists. The damaged young girl also falls to her knees, uncharacteristically bowing her head in deference to Nicnevin.

"Mercy, Goddess." Pivona's broken request is a low croak. She's dying to look at The Dark Queen but won't risk it. She knows she is in grave danger. Her intuition is firing at an all-time high. Her old crow friends lay in a paralyzed stupor all around her, not dead, but like Jenna McCray, not living.

Lead her to Delevan House. She is the blood of the seven years. I will level the village of Badb to a smoldering pit of endless human suffering if anyone has the stupidity to defy their Queen. Nicnevin raises an inhumanly long finger; her talons are sharp, blackened hooks that would decapitate without hesitation if she chooses to grant a merciful death. There would be no mercy on this night.

Rodger McDonald, with his wife and young son, lay in pieces, their bodies ripped apart and limbs scattered. Their bodies are unidentifiable as once being human. Terrified, they had tried to flee, an ill-fated decision. Two of the Sluagh attacked them and now feasted greedily on their flesh—sucking the marrow from the bones and intensely watching for others who would attempt to escape the nightmare of the insatiable Wild Hunt.

"Goddess. I ask permission." Caoimhe, once again in human form, stands tall before Nicnevin, confident in her plea. "She is the reason the Sutherland Coldiron failed. She snatched Grant's love from me. She blinded him. He chose to dishonor Badb and his family's obligation because of her. She is the reason the binding will not hold. The iron was contaminated because of this ignorant outsider. I do not mean to disrespect my Dark Queen, Nicnevin; I speak the truth. You have my loyalty and my oath as my kin. I would have her life." Backing away slowly, she moves to where Jenna lies helpless. "Her death will be a mercy now, and I request vengeance for her wrongs against me, your daughter's daughter, your blood." Her self-serving embellishment of the truth is convincing. Caoimhe lifts the necklace around her neck as evidence of her name, reminding the Goddess who she is. A Delevan.

The green stone is alive, pulsing with her mother's thirst. The stone calls to its mistress like a siren. Caoimhe's neck is smeared with drops of phantom blood.

Nicnevin waves her hand dismissively. The gesture is both condescending and accepting. Caoimhe sneers at the suffering villagers—some will never recover from this night, but they owe a debt. The cat-sìth's green eyes narrow to slits of bloodlust as she shifts her form again, this time for all to see.

She's done skulking in the shadows; her Unseelie kin now surround Caoimhe Delevan, and she can show her true self like never before. She pulls off her thin dress, flinging it to the ground. Her nude alabaster body is slim yet muscular, reflecting under the light of the moon peeking from behind the cracks at the entrance forced open by the Unseelie. The pendant around her neck glimmers with dark magick, covering her with a green shadow. She throws up her arms, flaunting herself on full display. What mortals regard as a monster is her gift. Caoimhe calls forth her beast. It's been pacing within, restlessly biding time until it can feed. Minor releases are not enough on this night of intense magicks in the divine presence of The Daughter of Frenzy. Her body tears open, and hot blood spatters over her feet and the thirsty earth. She leans into the shift with complete freedom and with the same abandon as an orgasm. She screams when the cat rips through her insides, turning her human body inside out. After stretching and taking pleasure in her feline form, the beast snarls, pouncing on Jenna McCray. The victim's mind is in shreds, and her body is already brutalized beyond repair from the molten metal. She accepts her inevitable fate.

"No more death!" Kieran Campbell takes a step forward.

Caoimhe snarls and hisses, loud and blood-chilling. Her claws are protracted razor weapons—lethal, and a single swipe of her oversized paw freezes the brave young man in place. She turns her attention back to her prize and effortlessly rips off Jenna's head. As soon as it hits the ground, Caoimhe is on it, slurping her blood. Her fangs gnash together, glowing huge and white. She purrs deeply, chewing on the seared flesh of the unfortunate young girl.

When she is sated, Caoimhe's form ripples; her cat-sìth turns inside out, revealing her sleek human shape once again, drenched in her own gore. Thin streaks of tears shine on her sculpted cheekbones. She's clutching the pendant tightly.

"Mother. I gift her blood and the blood of Badb to you."

The dreadful scene on the land of Badb is minor compared to the spectacle in the sky.

The heavens are morphing into a cloak of pitch-black dread. Even the stars have retreated behind a wall of suffocating silence. Delevan House is the only source of illumination, reverberating and alive with the essence of the souls trapped within. Souls who beg for retribution and release. Pieces of the ornate ironwork framing the structure begin to give way, cracking in place—parts of the cage meld into themselves and drop with an acid hiss into the water. The metal moans, and the rumble pierces the night.

The villagers of Badb are powerless against the torment among and enveloping them. An elderly woman, Robert

DELEVAN HOUSE

Gordon's grandmother, collapses dead to the ground, her heart exploding in terror.

Nicnevin's imposing male escort in black chainmail ascends with the body of The Threnody, leaving the Sluagh to protect his Goddess.

You will escort the girl. Nicnevin is translucent. She nods at Cameron Morven, but he's non-responsive. Even with the Dark Queen's command piercing his mind. His death is imminent. *I will take this man.* Her words penetrate the minds of those nearest to Cameron. Ever the bully, Robert Gordon pushes the handsome youth with thick waves of dark hair and delicate features hard on the back. Cameron clenches his fist, intending to strike Robert, but Marcus Gordon grabs his arm in support of his brother.

"Move. Or I'll kill you myself." Robert's arrogant courage is at an end.

Cameron apprehensively positions himself next to Pivona, taking her by the arm. Even now, she is cunning and seductive, and the mess of a girl leans into him protectively. Cameron has nothing left to lose, so he comforts her. He's hoping his death will be merciful as the Goddess worms her intentions through him.

I'm weary of cursed Badb. Walk. Nicnevin motions to the pair, driving them towards Delevan House. The flanking lochs are now a murky tar, roiling and churning. The stench of its life belched ashore is overpowering. *Walk. The blood oath is due post-haste. In physical presence, I return in seven years. Without Sutherland iron, there will be no mercy from the Sluagh for Badb if the village still stands, unrepentant and unwilling. My Wild*

NATASHA SINCLAIR AND RUTHANN JAGGE

Hunt will have their ways, breaking more than your feeble mortal bodies. Your flesh is nothing but a snack to my Faerie Host.

Her message echoes inside them all. With her warning, a bullet of agony shoots through every heart, leaving each villager breathless.

The gigantic Kelpie nudges Cameron Morven towards the walkway leading to Delevan House. The beast stumbles on the rocks, letting out a howl of frustration. Cameron freezes. The terrified young man takes one of Pivona's hands in his while looking directly into her once-sparkling eyes, now dull and pathetic.

"If you've got any traveller magick left in you, girl, now is the time to use it," Cameron whispers. "You deserve this, but I don't." Pivona shakes her head, and her feet refuse to move as fast as her brain. The fingers of her other hand are tight, straining to hold onto the yew seeds that Minerva Morven pushed between them. *Oh, I have magick, but I'm keeping what I have for myself.*

True to her nature, even under duress, Pivona doesn't offer to share Minerva's comfort with the young man. "I have no magick left in me. My family does, but they abandoned me. I curse them and this wretched village." Pivona's words slur. She slobbers from her swollen split tongue, though her pace suddenly quickens. "I will walk alone to my death, as I have through this miserable life." She drops Cameron's hand, shoving him away.

"No, take my hand Pivona!" Cameron raises his voice, trying to sound brave, above the rising sounds of honking geese. His throat tightens, and his heart quickens. As Pivona marches onwards, he's surrounded by the ghastly gaggle,

DELEVAN HOUSE

honking chaotically. They pluck at him, shredding his garments and skin. The smell of his blood whips them into a frenzy.

Cameron terror choked. His steps falter to a halt, not knowing which way to move. His flesh flays as the unholy transformation begins. The young man is swept into the air, arms flailing—claimed by Queen Nicnevin for her guard.

Cameron's cries echo over Badb, amplifying the carnage. Heather Morven screams inconsolably when her brother is ripped from this world to become one of the terrible Sluagh na marbh.

The villagers scatter as the Dark Queen and her raving and shrieking entourage soak out of sight into the darkness, disappearing into the ether high above Delevan House.

Robert Gordon tries to assure the horror-stricken villagers that all will be well, but no one is listening.

The brazen gypsy-teen squares her thin shoulders, pulling herself up to her petite height. She instinctively braids a lock of protection into her hair. Balancing on the tips of her toes, Pivona McQueeney dance-walks towards the gloom of Delevan House. *This isn't so bad. I'll finally be living in a fine house.*

The waters are calm. Displaced corvids shake their feathers, then rise from the ground, squawking in protest, then swooping boldly. They fill the sky, dancing in a perfectly choreographed waltz as they circle up to the apex of Delevan House.

Despite all she's endured, Pivona's brazen confidence remains intact. *I see you, my friends. Are you waiting for me?* Nearing the glorious and foreboding structure, the girl is eerily aware of the immense gargoyle, shadowed against the remnants of the Blue Moon, with his eyes of stone—watching.

Pivona shivers, wrapping her arms tightly around herself to steady fraying nerves. She wipes strands of damp hair away from her face. With a deep inhale, she squints, trying to see the masculine sculpture more clearly through the tacky salt mist surrounding the House. Her body tightens. *Is that sculpture smirking?*

Lady Delevan's familiar, Fraoch, appears in front of her. The unnaturally large bird's blackness is consuming, his stare soulless and eternal. He is flanked on either side by dozens of raven-black crows—hovering in the air, waiting for his command.

"You're a big one. What say you?" Pivona's apprehension fades as she wiggles a finger, beckoning the bird closer. Her mouth opens in shock at the creature appearing behind her familiar.

Lenore Delevan. The Immortal Baobhan Sìth. The Lady of Delevan House. *My Goddess.*

Her movement is stilted and stiff as she moves towards Pivona, defying the flow of the splendid emerald silk gown she wears. Jutting like sticky frames on a movie reel. Her black hair falls below her waist, mimicking the feathers of her flock. Precisely cobbled slippers of green velvet conceal her cloven feet, and her skin is pearly gray; the color of death. Delicate lines of hunger and fatigue etch the skin under her eyes. She was a great beauty before the wrath of Badb's ancestors mangled her—that is clear.

DELEVAN HOUSE

Pivona gasps. She can see past the horror. The Lady's seductive allure rests just beneath the surface. *My Goddess. I am yours.*

Lady Delevan's magnetic eyes are gleaming pools of emerald light in the fog surrounding the house; utterly hypnotic. Those marbled orbs are endlessly deep, reflecting centuries of suffering, a somber parade of the lives she led and the trials that trapped her.

She gazes, unblinking, into Pivona's eyes. The teen's blood runs cold.

The girl makes the sign of the cross and then folds her fingers into a sign of protection. She pops the mulch of now sweaty yew seeds into her mouth. They are sticky, warm and strangely comforting. Pivona winces, eyes watering from the sour taste, but the girl welcomes the warmth rushing through her body. Lady Delevan reaches out with a graceful hand to caress the side of her face.

"You are weary, Pivona, dear abandoned child." Lenore's voice is melodious, floating like one of her crows. "I'm hungry for life, much like you. I will ease your burden, and you will fly high, as you've always dreamed." Pivona's head is pounding, and her knees threaten to buckle from her as the Lady's vampiric essence floods her senses. The poison of a few yew berries is no match for the desire and power of this ancient creature.

The girl surrenders with a final sigh when the Lady in Green sinks her sharp teeth into Pivona McQueeney's jugular. Her surrender assures a painless bloodletting. It's *a good death and an easier one than I deserve.*

For the first time in seven years, Lady Delevan feeds. The young girl's rich, unpolluted blood is enough to imbue her with a little energy, taking the edge off her complex and insatiable hunger.

Her fading strength returns little by little with each swallow of Pivona's sweet life source, and within minutes, the girl's body is a husk. Every drop of her young blood now courses through the thirsty veins of the Baobhan Sìth.

When she releases the corpse, it falls to the ground, and the ornate iron fencing on either side twists and shakes. Eager to please their mistress, the crows nibble and peck at Pivona's body. Her corpse is covered in a flurry of black wings as her feathered friends absorb the remnants of her soul, stripping her flesh from the bones. When they are finished, another small corvid flutters its shiny black plumage under the watchful wings of the mature flock. Its first cry is a quiet but high-pitched twittering caw. *Finally, I'm part of their family.*

Lady Lenore Delevan is fed, but this failure of Badb's villagers to complete the binding ritual necessary to hold her captive within the walls of Delevan House and the proximity of her long-lost precious jewel sets her free. The Lady of Delevan House will roam for the first time since her trial in 1667.

Caoimhe Delevan stands alone on the shoreline of the village of Badb, clutching the pendant that cost Jenna McCray, Grant Sutherland, and the others their lives. She's watching for a sign, fully aware that the binding ritual obligating the village of Badb has not been fulfilled. Mauve perches lightly on her shoulder, pressing her pink beak into Caoimhe's cheek in a corvid kiss. The brilliant turquoise eyes of her white crow are sharp. When the bird senses Lady Delevan's approach, she caws a greeting, flapping her wings in excitement.

DELEVAN HOUSE

Gliding smoother now, her strength boosted by rare gypsy blood, Lady Delevan floats inches above the barnacle-covered wood as she moves along the duckboard walkway, connecting Delevan House to the village of Badb.

Caoimhe wraps her fingers tightly around the green stone around her neck. The magnificent jewel glows hot, almost searing Caoimhe's palm. She presses the gem against her chest. It's heavier now, and tears shimmer as it burns an impression of its crescent and V-rod deep into her skin.

She's coming. Removing the fiery pendant around her neck, she turns from the loch inland.

The wings of Lenore Delevan's flock cover Caoimhe in protection as she heads toward the bank. The Lady's power calls to her. Her siren's song rises. The sound of it is louder now, carried by the water, in a melody only she can hear.

When Caoimhe finally sees her, she falls to her knees. She bows her head, holding the necklace outstretched towards The Lady in Green.

Mother.

Epilogue

After 353 years of confinement to Delevan House, with only a single blood offering every 7 years, Lady Lenore Delevan was finally free. The residents of Badb came face to face with the Dark Queen, Nicnevin and her terrible Wild Hunt, the Sluagh na marbh. Blood had spilled. Souls had been claimed.

Badb would never be the same again.

The Lady's daughter, Caoimhe Delevan, helped restore her power by offering her the pendant bestowed upon The Lady when she was gifted her immortality. Caoimhe paid a terrible price in losing her true love on that grisly night of the Samhain Blue Moon.

Minerva Morven stands on the shoreline, watching dawn break over the village. Her heart is grave with the sacrifice of her nephew, Cameron Morven, to the Dark Queen, and she's missing her son, Arlen.

Feeling her age, Minerva rakes through the smoldering coals of Badb's fire, bending to collect shards of bone. She will use them to honor their deaths in her unique way. Some will be sprinkled on the ground in spring to encourage a good harvest. Her sewing circle gathers what remains of the bodies of Jenna and the others. Prayers are uttered for their souls, and their remains are consumed by the flames. The ashes will be gathered, then committed to the North Sea to rest among the waves.

Minerva notices a large cloud of dust sparkling on the horizon in the dawning light. A long caravan of wagons snakes through the tree line. Heading towards Badb. Word travels quickly through rural communities, and the corvids in the sky above circle slowly.

They are watching. Always.

The consequence of Lady Delevan's freedom is unimaginable. Will the Travellers demand retribution and revenge for the death of Pivona McQueeney, one of their own, who was sacrificed? Their magicks are ancient, and like the community of Badb, they don't adhere to the laws of most either. The relentless torment of a gypsy curse may be powerful enough to rival the evil of Badb.

Minerva Morven will need all her powers for what's to come.

Note from the Authors

Delevan House has been big, beautiful journey for both writers. Every detail was discussed at length, and then some. Crossing time zones in video meetings, emails and DMs, we learned much from one other in the form and fusion of our collective visions for this novel. When it came to language, that too was discussed, and as with our separate styles, we opted for a blended approach.

Delevan House is the creation of an American author and a Scottish author, with a setting that also crosses between these two countries and languages.

While at the core of Delevan House, the primary language is English. It cannot go unacknowledged that there is no such thing as a single English. More accurately, English is a global variety of Englishes. English is a lingua franca that brings many linguistic backgrounds together. The use of Englishes bridges cultures.

There may be an expectation for a novel by two such writers to choose between a standard form of either British or American English. Depending on which form you're most exposed to in literature, you may have noticed we have taken on board Standard American English spellings for much of the novel. Except for dialogue which must always reflect the culture and authentic vocabulary of the characters, most of which are Scottish. Therefore, dialogue is executed by harnessing a mix of Englishes (American and British), some Scots, and some light Gaelic. Thus, our approach is,

DELEVAN HOUSE

grammatically and stylistically, descriptive and absolutely not outdated and static prescriptive.

Given that we do work with two minority languages within our folk horror, if curious readers not familiar with Scots or Scottish Gaelic would like to explore these languages a little further then, www.dsl.ac.uk[1] is a great online dictionary for Scots and www.learngaelic.scot[2] is a great resource to explore Scottish Gaelic.

We are keen to share this merging of cultures through our collaborative brazen folk horror with a global readership, authentically and respectfully, by embracing language and cultural diversity. Hours are spent researching and comparing notes. We borrow inspiration, as all speculative work does, but stay rooted in the past. You could easily infer that we've gone rogue! And we own our temperament with a fierce passion for bringing readers a contemporary reading experience in folk horror.

We discussed whether or not to include a glossary since this book may introduce some readers to snippets of unfamiliar language and beings of Celtic folklore. Ultimately, we decided to direct you to follow Brazen Folk Horror.

This book is the beginning of the worlds we will share with readers! Our progress will be complemented with articles and features of interest on the website designed just for you. As storytellers, we'll take your hand and dive deep below the surface. To coin a phrase from, an author we both greatly respect Clive Barker, 'We have such sights to show you.'

We truly do.

---

1. https://dsl.ac.uk/
2. https://learngaelic.scot/index.jsp

If you would love to learn more about how this first collaboration between Jagge and Sinclair came to be, please visit 'The Making of Delevan House' on our site, Brazen Folk Horror[3] and follow our adventures as we continue the Delevan Trilogy with Book II: *The Delevan Diaries*, releasing in 2023.

---

3. https://brazenfolkhorror.com/

What Did You Think?

Please consider leaving an honest review of this and any of our other works you have read. Reviews can be submitted easily via various online platforms. It takes only seconds and every single one matters in helping other readers decide whether to take a chance and read for themselves. They really are vital, particularly for indie authors, editors and publishers.

Thank you.

About the Authors

Ruthann Jagge and Natasha Sinclair were strangers who met through publishers while writing from their respective desks in Texas and Scotland. They have shared pages in numerous successful anthologies and collections. Well-received solo work amplifies their unique voices.

Through this connection, a friendship blossomed from a shared passion for crafting compelling, multidimensional characters and uncovering dark stories hiding in the shadows.

These two authors deeply respect history and are passionate about the magical and macabre.

The stories of Jagge and Sinclair have roots in folklore passed through the generations by great storytellers, both in verbal and written forms.

This pair enjoys sinking their claws deep into horror realism, legends, and mysticism without boundaries.

The fearless duo has joined forces to collaborate on shamelessly original and wicked tales readers crave. The Brazen Folk Horror tag is #BeBrazen

Brazen Folk Horror[1]

---

1. https://brazenfolkhorror.com/

DELEVAN HOUSE

THE DELEVAN DIARIES

JAGGE & SINCLAIR

NATASHA SINCLAIR AND RUTHANN JAGGE